"Hello, Diane?  **just made the b myself."**

"No, it's Toby. Diane isn't home."

"Toby? I'm sorry. I thought—"

"Julie, you sound terrible. What's the matter?"

"Oh. Nothing."

"Nothing? How can you sound so bad about nothing?"

"It's nothing. Really. It's about a boy."

"Well, I'm a boy."

"Toby, I know you're a boy."

"So maybe I can help."

"Don't be ridiculous."

"Well, thanks for the vote of confidence, Julie."

"Where's Diane?"

"I don't know. Out having her ears glued down."

"Toby! Stop that! You know how sensitive Diane is about her big ears. You're just being a pig."

"Oink-oink."

"Goodbye. I'm going to hang up now."

"Break my heart."

Books by R. L. Stine

Fear Street: THE NEW GIRL
Fear Street: THE SURPRISE PARTY
Fear Street: THE OVERNIGHT
Fear Street: MISSING
Fear Street: THE WRONG NUMBER
Fear Street: THE SLEEPWALKER

HOW I BROKE UP WITH ERNIE
PHONE CALLS

Available from ARCHWAY Paperbacks

PHONE CALLS

R.L. Stine

AN ARCHWAY PAPERBACK
Published by POCKET BOOKS
New York   London   Toronto   Sydney   Tokyo   Singapore

For Jane, who actually liked this one

AN ARCHWAY PAPERBACK *Original*

An Archway Paperback published by
POCKET BOOKS, a division of Simon & Schuster Inc.
1230 Avenue of the Americas, New York, NY 10020

ISBN: 0-671-69497-9

First Archway Paperback printing June 1990

10 9 8 7 6 5 4 3 2 1

AN ARCHWAY PAPERBACK and colophon are
registered trademarks of Simon & Schuster Inc.

Printed in the U.S.A.

IL 6+

CHAPTER 1

Diane Calls Julie

"Hello."

"Hello. Julie?"

"No. It's her mom. Is this Diane?"

"Yes. Hi, Mrs. Reynolds. Is Julie there?"

"She'd better be. It's after eleven o'clock. Isn't it a little late to be calling, Diane?"

"Eleven. Oh, wow. My watch must've stopped. It says nine o'clock. Do you believe it?"

"No. Not really. Never mind. I'll go get Julie."

"Hello?"

"Hi, Julie. It's me. What are you doing?"

"My nails."

"What color?"

"Well, I don't know. I was thinking about purple. Or maybe black."

"Have you thought about blue? Maybe you could find a shade to match your eyes. I've always thought it would be neat to have eyes and nails that match."

"You're weird, Diane. Actually, I never do anything to my nails at all, except chew on them. But sometimes I think about doing something to them. That's what I was doing when you called. Thinking about doing something to them."

"Do you want something better to think about?"

"Yeah. Sure."

"Well—how about Mick?"

"Mick?"

"Yeah. Mick."

"Diane, why should I think about Mick?"

"Well, from what I just heard, he's been thinking about *you.*"

"Get real, Diane."

"I'm serious. I was talking to Carol Trager, and she said her brother told her Mick thinks you're neat. He likes girls with very curly blond hair."

"But, Diane, Mick doesn't know me."

"Carol seemed to think he *wants* to know you!"

"But he's a junior. I've never spoken a word to him. He's never even said hello to me."

"Well, he's really shy, Julie."

"He's shy? I don't see what that has to—"

"You're kinda shy, too. You two have a lot in common. I think you should call him."

"Call him? Get real. I couldn't call him. What would I say?"

"I don't know. Ask him something. Ask him what it's like to be a junior."

"Don't be a dork."

Ask him if you can interview him for the school paper."

"But I don't work on the school paper."

"He doesn't know that."

"No. Really—I couldn't—"

"Wow. It's a great idea. You pretend to interview him, and I know he'll ask you out. Carol says he really wants to ask you out. He just needs an excuse."

"But, Diane. I couldn't. I can't."

"My brother has a little cassette player. You could bring it over to Mick's to tape the interview. That'll really impress him."

"But what happens when the school paper comes out and the interview isn't in it? He'll know I was a fake!"

"By that time, you two will be going together. He'll be so nuts about you, he won't care. Trust me, Julie, this is a perfect plan."

"If it's so perfect, why do I feel so weird about it?"

"Because you're a chicken, Julie."

"Thanks for the compliment."

"What are friends for? Listen, you have no choice. You've *got* to do this. Carol says the guy is really hot for you. At least that's what her brother told her."

"Who's her brother? The guy with all the teeth?"

"Yeah. That's him. Carol says he wants to have his teeth straightened, but no one can figure out which way they should go."

"How awful."

"Yeah. She's embarrassed to be seen with him, but she feels sorry for him, too. He's her brother, after all."

3

"And he and Mick are friends?"

"I guess so. Listen, Julie, are you going to call Mick or not?"

"I don't know. I can't decide. I don't think I— Listen, Diane, I've got to get off the phone. My mom is screaming at me from downstairs."

"Okay. See you tomorrow."

"Right. Oh. Wait. Diane?"

"Yeah?"

"What's the name of the school paper?"

"Hmmmm—I think it's *The Beacon.* I'm not sure."

"Thanks. Good night."

CHAPTER 2

Julie Calls Mick

"Hello. Mick?"

"Hello. You have reached the Wilson family, but no one is here to answer your call. Please leave a message when you hear the beep, and we'll call you back as soon as we can. Thanks for calling. Remember to wait for the beep."

Beeeep.

"Oh. Hi. I wanted to—well—you probably don't know me but . . . Well, maybe you do. I wanted to—uh—I'm not being too clear here. I guess I'll call you back later. Sorry, I mean—bye."

CHAPTER 3

Julie Calls Diane

"Hello, Diane? It's me. I just made the biggest fool of myself."

"No. It's Toby. Diane isn't home."

"Toby? I'm sorry. I just thought Diane would answer. She always does."

"Julie, you sound terrible. What's the matter?"

"Oh, nothing."

"Nothing? How can you sound so bad about nothing?"

"It's nothing. Really. It's about a boy."

"Well, I'm a boy."

"Toby, I know you're a boy."

"So maybe I can help."

"Don't be ridiculous."

"Well, thanks for the vote of confidence, Julie."

"Don't get insulted, Toby. Do you know Mick Wilson?"

"The basketball player?"

"Yeah."

"We're in the same gym class. He's always a team captain. When he chooses sides, he never chooses me."

"Sorry, Toby, but it's kind of funny, thinking of you and him in the same gym class."

"Stop laughing, Julie. I think I'm going to get really steamed if you don't stop laughing."

"Well, admit it. You're not exactly the jock type."

"Oh, really? Have you ever seen me with a tennis racquet in my hand?"

"No."

"That's because I don't play tennis."

"Oh."

"You can laugh at that, Julie. That was a joke."

"Oh."

"Listen. Just because Mick Wilson can run, dribble, and shoot from anywhere on the floor doesn't make him a great athlete, either."

"Toby, you sound positively jealous."

"Shut up."

"Listen to you."

"Just shut up."

"Make me."

"Why do you want to know about Mick Wilson?"

"None of your business, Toby."

"None of my business? But you brought him up! You asked me about him!"

"I told you you couldn't help me."

7

"You're right. You're beyond help!"

"You don't have to scream at me. You're not *my* brother. You're Diane's. You're supposed to scream at her."

"She isn't here. And she isn't the one who's driving me crazy."

"How come we always fight?"

"I'm not fighting, Julie. I'm the shrimpy little nerd who shouldn't be in the same gym class with Mick Wilson. So how can I fight?"

"Come off it. I didn't mean that as an insult. Lighten up, okay? Where's Diane?"

"I don't know. Out having her ears glued down."

"Toby! Stop that! You know how sensitive Diane is about her big ears. You shouldn't tease her about her ears."

"Then what should I tease her about?"

"You're just being a pig."

"Oink-oink."

"Goodbye. I'm going to hang up now."

"Break my heart."

"Tell Diane I called, okay? No. Don't tell her. Tell her it wasn't important."

"Okay. I'll tell her you didn't call and it wasn't important."

"Very funny. Remind me to laugh."

"Bye, Julie."

"Bye. Oh, Toby?"

"Yeah?"

"Do you have your notes for Miller's chemistry exam?"

"Of course."

"Can I borrow them from you?"

"Of course. Don't you always?"

"Yes. I guess I do. Thanks, Toby. See you."

"See you, Julie."

===== CHAPTER 4 =====

Julie Calls Mick

=======

"Hello."

"Hello, Mick?"

"No. You do not have the pleasure of speaking to Mick. This is his humble visitor Ramar."

"What?"

"I said, you do not have the pleasure of speaking to—"

"Oh. Ramar. Yes. I've heard about you."

"As they say in my country, bad news travels fast on a windy day. Ha-ha!"

"You're the foreign exchange student who's living with Mick's family this year."

"I am liking your voice. Do you know my country?"

"No. I—"

"It is bright yellow."

"Your country is yellow?"

"Only on the map. Not in real life."

"Oh. Uh—interesting. That's very interesting, Ramar. Is Mick home?"

"Yes, he resides here presently."

"Well, could I speak to him?"

"Could you or may you? Hee-hee."

"Is that a joke?"

"It is what I call a pleasantry."

"May I speak to Mick?"

"With pleasure I am turning over the receiver to him."

"Hello?"

"Hello, Mick?"

"Yeah."

"This is Julie. Julie Reynolds."

"Yeah?"

"It's not too late to call, is it?"

"Too late? It's five o'clock in the afternoon!"

"Oh. Right. Well . . ,"

"I'm sorry. Who is this? There's a lot of noise here. Ramar is playing the bagpipes or something. I didn't catch your name."

"It's Julie. Julie Reynolds."

"Are you from school?"

"What? Yes. I'm in Miss Joffry's homeroom."

"Yeah?"

"Well—uh—you're probably wondering why I'm calling."

"Yeah."

"Well, I'm calling because—"

"Hey—Reynolds. Wasn't your brother on the wrestling team? He was all-state or something, and then his arm got bent."

"No. I don't have a brother."

"Oh. But do you know who I mean? Big guy with a red face? Used to wear bright red sweaters? Always looked so weird walking around with a bent arm?"

"No. I didn't know him. I'm a sophomore. I mean, I'm not into wrestling."

"Yeah?"

"I go to all the basketball games, though."

"Yeah?"

"I guess you're still wondering why I called."

"Yeah."

"Well, I'd like to—uh, interview you."

"Me?"

"Yeah. For the school paper, *The Beacon.* I think that's what it's called."

"You want to interview me?"

"Yeah. I mean, yes. Would you mind if—"

"But they just interviewed me. Last week."

"They did?"

"Yeah. Chris Murdoch. You know Chris?"

"Sure. Of course I know him."

"He already interviewed me for *The Beacon.*"

"Oh. Right. I knew that. It's just that—uh—well, Chris lost his notes."

"He did?"

"Yeah. So he asked me to do a follow-up. You know. Try to piece together the stuff he lost."

"Oh."

"So, do you think you might have time?"

"Yeah."

"When? I mean—"

"Well, I have basketball practice at seven-thirty. You could come over before. Say seven."

"Come over to your house?"

"Yeah."

"Oh. Okay. That's good. It shouldn't take long. Thanks, Mick. See you at seven."

"Yeah."

"Well, bye."

"Oh, Judy? Do you know my address?"

"It's Julie. Yes. I live just a few blocks away, across Fremont by the playground."

"Yeah?"

"See you later, Mick. Thanks."

"Bye."

CHAPTER 5
Mick Calls Toby

"Hello."

"Hello, Toby?"

"No. This is his dad. Who's this?"

"A friend of his."

"Oh. Hold on. I'll get him. Isn't this a little late to be calling?"

"Yeah. I guess. I just got home from basketball practice."

"I see. Hold on."

"Hello?"

"Toby?"

"Speaking."

"It's Mick Wilson. How ya doin'?"

"Mick? Hi. What's happening?"

"Not much. I just wanted to ask you about that girl."

"Girl? What girl?"

"Come on, man. I'm onto your little joke."

"Mick, I really don't know what you're talking about."

"Yeah. Sure."

"What girl?"

"The girl you sent over to my house. Julie Reynolds."

"Julie? I sent Julie to your house?"

"Come on, Toby. What's the joke? I don't get it."

"I don't get it, either, Mick. Julie's a friend of mine. Actually, she's my sister's friend. But I didn't send her over to your house. Why would I do that?"

"I don't know."

"She was at your house tonight?"

"Yeah."

"Well, what makes you think I sent her?"

"She told me."

"She what?"

"She told me you sent her, Toby."

"But that's impossible."

"I don't get it, man. Were you trying to embarrass me or something?"

"No. I—"

"Then I don't get it."

"I don't get it, either."

"Maybe she's bananas, or something."

"Maybe."

"She *must* be bananas because I think she's after your bod, Toby."

"What?"

"The way she kept talking about you. She's after your bod, man."

"That's stupid, Mick."

"Yeah. I know."

"Well, you don't have to get insulting."

"I think she's hot for you, man. She's not bad looking, either. I'd ask her out myself if I wasn't going with Sarah—and Jenny."

"This is some kind of put-on, right? Julie just barely tolerates me. Every time we talk, we get into some kind of a fight."

"Sounds like true love, Toby."

"No way, Mick. No way this makes any sense."

"Tell me about it. She said you told her to come see me. I don't get it, man. I don't get the joke."

"It must be some kind of a mix-up."

"Yeah."

"I'll bet my sister had something to do with it. Diane and Julie are best friends. But it wasn't me. Really."

"Yeah."

"No. You've got to believe me!"

"Whatever you say, man. I've got to get some shut-eye. I'm whipped, man. Coach was in a bad mood tonight, and when he's in a bad mood, we do laps. Lots of laps."

"Too bad."

"Yeah."

"Well, okay. See you around, Mick."

"Not if I see you first. Ha-ha!"

"Funny."

"Hey, Toby—one other thing."

PHONE CALLS

"What's that?"

"Do you have notes for Miller's chemistry exam?"

"Yes."

"Can I borrow them?"

"I guess so."

"Thanks, man. See ya."

"See ya."

CHAPTER 6
Julie Calls Toby

"Hello."

"Hello, Diane?"

"No. It's Toby."

"Good. Because I was calling to tell Diane I'm never speaking to her again."

"Julie, chill out. Chill out! You're shouting in my ear."

"Just tell her. Okay? Tell her I'm never speaking to her again, and I'm never thinking about her again, and I'm never calling her again."

"I think I get the idea. Will you stop shouting? What's your problem?"

"Problem? What's my problem? Just that your sister got me into the most embarrassing, the most humiliating, the most unspeakably unspeakable night of my life!"

"Julie, I'm sure there's some mistake. Diane's your friend."

"Diane *was* my friend. I can't believe it, Toby. I can't believe what she did to me! I'll never live it down. I'll carry the embarrassment to my grave."

"Julie, what—"

"I just gave myself an idea. Hold on. I'm going to jump out the window."

"What room are you in?"

"The den."

"The den is on the first floor."

"I know, but maybe I'll fall into the rosebushes and bleed to death from the thorns."

"Julie, please. Just chill out. Tell me what happened."

"I might as well tell you. It'll be all over school tomorrow. How can I go to school? How can I ever face anyone again? Everyone will know what an idiot I am. I made a perfect fool of myself."

"No one's perfect. Ha-ha!"

"Shut up, Toby. Do you want to hear what Diane did to me or not?"

"Sure. Tell me, Julie."

"She told me that Mick Wilson wanted to ask me out, but he was too shy."

"Mick? Shy?"

"She said if I made up an excuse and went over to see him, he'd ask me out because he really wanted to."

"So you made up an excuse and went over there?"

"How'd you guess?"

"Julie—really."

"Save your sarcasm for the end, Toby. It gets a lot worse. Ack! Why am I telling you all this?"

"Because I'm just Diane's brother Toby, and it doesn't matter what I think of you?"

"I guess. Anyway—"

"Thanks, pal."

"Oh, don't start a fight now. I can't take any more. Really. Just shut up and listen. I went over to Mick's before practice tonight and pretended I was interviewing him for the school paper."

"The Bugle?"

"It's called *The Bugle?* I thought it was called *The Beacon!* Oh, no. Oh, wow—"

"Go on, Julie. Don't keep me in suspense."

"You'd better not enjoy this story, Toby. Or I'll never speak to you again, either."

"Could I have that in writing?"

"Stop it. Just shut up. I borrowed your cassette player from Diane to make it look like I was getting the interview on tape."

"Get to the good part, Julie. Did he ask you out?"

"Oh, for sure. That's why I'm in such a great mood! Have you lost your brain? No, he didn't ask me out. He wasn't the least bit interested in me. He didn't know who I was. He didn't recognize me at all. Everything Diane said was a lie."

"So what did you do?"

"What could I do? I was so embarrassed and nervous. I kept asking myself, 'What am I doing here?' I had no choice. I had to go through with the interview."

"And?"

"And your stupid sister hadn't given me any tape. So there I was. I turned on the cassette player. I pushed Play and Record, and I tried to think of a question to ask him. Then he started to laugh. He laughed so hard, he fell off the couch. He couldn't breathe."

"Because he saw you didn't have a cassette in the recorder?"

"Yes. Hey, don't you start laughing."

"I'm not. So, go on. He laughed so hard he couldn't breathe. What did you do? Give him mouth-to-mouth?"

"Don't be a pig. Sometimes you're really disgusting, Toby."

"Only sometimes? That's the nicest thing you ever said to me. Go on. What did you do?"

"I panicked. When I saw what he was laughing about, I just panicked. I turned off the recorder. I told him something about how I had a photographic memory, or something. I tried to go on with the interview. But—but—"

"But, what?"

"But I couldn't think of any questions to ask him."

"Oh, no."

"Oh, yes. It was horrible. My mind went blank. I just wanted to hide somewhere. I really thought about it, hiding behind the couch. He thought it was hilarious, the big, dumb jock. He thought it was some kind of practical joke. How could it be a practical joke? There I was, so embarrassed and mortified I was ready to hide behind the couch. How could it be a joke? He asked me whose idea it was."

"And you said—"

"I told him it was yours."

"Julie—"

"I'm sorry, Toby. I told you, my mind was a blank. Yours was the first name I could think of. I guess because you told me you're in his gym class. I'm really sorry. I just panicked and blurted out your name."

"Great. That's just great, Julie. When we have gym on Wednesday, he'll probably slam dunk me. That's Mick's idea of a practical joke!"

"No. I'm sure—"

"Did you say anything else about me to Mick?"

"What?"

"Did you tell him some other things about me?"

"No. That was it."

"I thought so. So he was putting me on."

"He—what? You mean he called you? He called you to say what a dork I am?"

"Uh, no. He didn't call, Julie. I—uh—was thinking of something else. Finish the story."

"There's nothing to finish. I told him to look for his interview in *The Beacon,* and I ran out of there as fast as I could. I can't believe I didn't even get the name of the paper right. Why did Diane do that to me, Toby? Why?"

"I don't know."

"Brilliant. You're supposed to be a brain. Come on. Tell me why she played such a horrible trick on me. She's your sister."

"Give me some slack, Julie. You know she's not my real sister. She's only my sister because my father married her mother."

"That's no excuse. Why did she do this to me?"

"Well, maybe it's because she's hot for Mick."

"What?"

"I think maybe I've heard her talking about him with some other girls. I think she finds him really interesting. And maybe sending you over there was a roundabout way of getting to know him."

"You mean she used me."

"It's just a wild guess, Julie. It's not a fact, or anything."

"She used me. She used me to get to Mick. What a mean trick."

"Well, we shouldn't jump to conclusions. I'm probably way off base. I shouldn't have—"

"Just tell her never to call me again, Toby. I've never heard of anything so low."

"Come on, Julie. You should give her a chance to exp—"

"Good night, Toby. I've got to get off the phone. I'm suddenly exhausted. I can't even hold the phone to my ear. I guess that's what total humiliation does to a person."

"Okay. Sorry you're so upset. Get some sleep. Oh, and please bring back my cassette recorder tomorrow, okay?"

"Oh. That's the other thing."

"Other thing?"

"Yeah. I ran out in such a panic, I left it at Mick's. Sorry, Toby."

"Good night, Julie. Thanks for everything."

"You don't have to be so sarcastic, do you? Well, do you?"

"I guess not."

"You know I'm in pain. You know I'll never be able to hold my head up or look anyone in the eye again. So don't be sarcastic. It's the least you can do."

"You're right, Julie. You're shouting again."

"Well, good night."

"Good night."

CHAPTER 7

Diane Calls Julie

"Hello?"

"Hello, Julie?"

"No, it's her mom. How are you, Diane?"

"Okay. Is Julie home?"

"Yes. Just a minute . . . Uh—Diane?"

"Yes?"

"Julie says she can't come to the phone right now."

"Tell her I just need to talk to her for a minute."

"Sorry, Diane. Julie says—uh—*Julie, I'm not going to tell Diane that! If you want to tell her, tell her yourself. But I think you're being very childish!*"

"Mrs. Reynolds—"

"*Julie, I'm not going to fight your fights for you. Why are you fighting with Diane, anyway?*"

"Mrs. Reynolds—"

"I'm sorry, Diane. I don't know what's going on between you two, but you're both mature young ladies. You're not kids anymore, and you should be able to solve your disagreements in a more grown-up manner."

"That's true, Mrs. Reynolds. I agree with you completely. Would you do me one favor?"

"What's that?"

"Tell Julie she's a stupid pinhead and her hair looks like a rat's nest in a hurricane."

"Goodbye, Diane."

"Goodbye, Mrs. Reynolds."

CHAPTER 8

Toby Calls Julie

"Hello?"

"Hello, Julie?"

"No, it's her mom. Hold on. I'll get her. Who is this?"

"Toby."

"Toby, what happened between Julie and Diane?"

"I don't know."

"You don't know? Julie won't tell us anything. But I can see she's terribly upset."

"They'll probably work it out, Mrs. Reynolds."

"You think so? Listen, Toby, it's none of my business, but you're Diane's brother. If there's anything you can do to help solve this——"

"I don't know. I'm not Diane's real brother. So she doesn't listen to me much. She's usually pretty nasty to me."

"She's nasty to you? That means she *does* think of you as a real brother!"

"Hmmmm. Maybe you're right, Mrs. Reynolds."

"Hold on, Toby. I'll get Julie."

"Hello?"

"Hello, Julie?"

"Who is this?"

"It's Mick. I just wondered if we could continue our interview this weekend. My parents are going away, and we'll be all alone the whole time."

"Toby, shut up! You don't sound anything like Mick!"

"Ha-ha! Sorry, Julie. I couldn't resist."

"I should just hang up. You're disgusting."

"Yeah, I know. Ha-ha!"

"I hate your laugh, too. You sound like Pee-wee Herman."

"Okay, okay. Don't start tearing me to pieces now. I just called to see how you were feeling."

"And you couldn't resist kicking me while I was down?"

"I didn't kick you. I made a little joke."

"It was in bad taste."

"I'm sorry. Okay?"

"Okay."

"So how are you?"

"I'm miserable. I've lost my best friend, and everywhere I go, people look at me with smirks on their faces and pretend they're not thinking about what a triple-dip bozo I am."

"Well, at least you're not getting paranoid."

"Did you call me up just to laugh at me?"

"No. I told you. I just wondered how you were doing. I'm your friend, remember?"

"Oh, yeah. I forgot."

"You sound terrible. When do you think you'll lighten up?"

"When I'm dead. Did Diane say anything to you?"

"No. She doesn't talk to me much. Usually, she just says, 'Get out of the bathroom!' That's mostly what she says to me. She has been weird the past two days, though. She seems very confused."

"Confused? Confused that I didn't enjoy her little practical joke?"

"I don't know. I think you should try to make up with her or something."

"Who asked you?"

"Nobody. But—"

"First I have to get my revenge."

"Revenge? Julie, have you gone bananas, or what?"

"I've been thinking about it a lot, Toby."

"About what?"

"About revenge. Will you help me?"

"Help you do what?"

"Get revenge, of course."

"Julie, she's my sister. I mean, I've got to live with her, remember?"

"I'm not asking you to do anything too horrendous. I just want to embarrass and humiliate Diane for life, the way she did me."

"Well, that sounds perfectly reasonable."

"I think you're being sarcastic again, Toby."

"You're not as dumb as you look."

"You think I look dumb?"

"Julie, don't sound so hurt. That's an expression. It doesn't mean anything. I'm sorry. I didn't know my opinion meant anything to you."

"It doesn't. Now do you want to hear my idea?"

"No. But go ahead."

"You tell Diane that you were talking to Mick in gym class and that Mick is nuts about Diane and wants Diane to call him."

"What? Are you serious?"

"Of course I'm serious."

"But why would Diane believe that?"

"You said she's got a crush on him, didn't you?"

"I said I thought *maybe* she has a crush on him."

"So, why won't she believe it?"

"Because she just pulled the same gag on you. She's not totally brain dead, you know."

"She'll fall for it."

"But it's the exact same joke."

"That's why she'll fall for it. Who would be stupid enough to try the exact same joke on someone?"

"But if Mick is so interested in Diane, why hasn't he called her himself? Why hasn't he come by her locker or something? Why does she have to call him?"

"Because deep down underneath, he's really very shy."

"Who would be stupid enough to believe that?"

"I was!"

"Oh. Right. Well, I don't know, Julie. If I do this, then you'll be even with Diane, and you'll make up with her?"

"Yes. Once she is humiliated for life and cannot show her face in school again, I'll be happy to make up with her."

"That sounds fair."

"Sarcasm, sarcasm. It's such a bad habit."

"I have a lot of bad habits. Want to hear about some others?"

"Don't be such a pig, Toby. And don't change the subject. Will you do this or not?"

"Well, I don't know. I guess I could do it. But only to put an end to this stupid fight between you two."

"You're a pal, Toby. Tell Diane that Mick drools all over her yearbook picture every night."

"She isn't going to buy it. She's going to figure out that it's a gag."

"If she really has a crush on him, she'll want to believe it. Make it seem real, Toby. Get a scrap of paper. Write, 'Please call me' on it. You know, in funny handwriting. Sign it 'Mick' and put his phone number on the bottom."

"I don't know, Julie. I can't—"

"Please, Toby. You want Diane and me to be friends again, don't you?"

"Well, sure. But—"

"So, you're not playing a dirty trick on Diane. You're doing her a favor. You're doing us all a favor."

"I guess—"

"After Diane's embarrassment and humiliation wear off in a year or so, we'll all be happy again— because of you."

"Well, if you put it that way . . ."

"You'll do it?"

"Yeah. Okay."

"Don't let me down, Toby. And let me know exactly what happens. Revenge isn't any good unless you hear all the juicy details."

"Good night, Julie."

"See ya."

═══ CHAPTER 9 ═══
Toby Calls Diane
───

"Hello?"

"Hello, Diane?"

"No. It's Francine. Who's this?"

"Toby. Can I talk to Diane?"

"Diane, it's your brother!"

"Toby?"

"Hi."

"What do you want? Why are you calling me at Francine's? We're studying for the chem exam."

"Well, I—"

"No. You can't listen to my tapes. You always put them back in the wrong boxes."

"Diane, I don't want to listen to your tapes, believe me. Barry Manilow gets me too excited."

"Give me a break, Toby. I have only *one* Barry Manilow tape! And it was a present from someone."

"You bought it for yourself, Diane, and you've listened to it, too."

"Not very often. At least I don't waste my money on all that heavy-metal trash, all those ugly guys in black leather wearing makeup and screaming like banshees. How come you only listen to groups with guys who wear makeup, Toby? Don't you think that's a little strange?"

"No, I don't, Diane. I think—"

"What do you want? You didn't call to discuss music, did you? Francine and I are trying to study."

"No. I called because I had some news I thought you'd want to hear."

"What's that? Your face cleared up? I'll hear about it on the eleven o'clock news."

"Stop laughing, Diane. That wasn't funny. And tell Francine to stop laughing, too."

"It was too funny."

"You know, I'm calling because I'm a good brother and I heard something I knew you'd be interested in. *Stop laughing!*"

"I'm sorry. *Stop laughing, Francine.* Okay, she stopped. What did you want to tell me?"

"Just this. I had gym class today—"

"And they asked you to be second base? Ha-ha-ha!"

"Stop it, Diane. Really. You're not funny. I'm trying to do you a favor, and all you do is—"

"Sorry. It's Francine. She's making me laugh. She just did the best imitation of you. She looked so serious and bookwormy."

"I give up."

"No. Come on, Toby. Lighten up."

"No. I give up."

34

"Don't be so dramatic. Just tell me why you called. I won't interrupt. I promise."

"I called because I had gym class this afternoon, and I was talking to Mick, and Mick said he really liked you, and he—"

"Mick Hardesty said he liked me? That's impossible."

"Mick Hardesty? No, Diane. Not Mick Hardesty. Mick Wilson."

"Mick Wilson the basketball player?"

"Yeah."

"Well, he doesn't know me."

"I guess he does. He said he thought you were neat. He gave me a note to give to you."

"Mick Wilson?"

"Yes."

"What does the note say?"

"Diane, I wouldn't read your personal notes."

"What does it say?"

"It says, 'Please call me. Mick.' And it's got his phone number on it."

"You're joking."

"No. I'm serious."

"He's got to be joking."

"I don't think so. Mick doesn't have much of a sense of humor. His idea of something funny is if some guy slams his hand in a locker door. That's about it."

"You're just putting him down because he likes me."

"Can you think of a better reason?"

"Read the note again, Toby."

"I don't have it. I put it on your dresser."

"You were in my room?"

"I just put the note on your dresser."

"Do you think I should call him tonight?"

"You could try, but I think he's got practice tonight."

"He really told you he thought I was neat?"

"Yeah. There's no accounting for taste."

"Why doesn't he call me?"

"I think he's kind of shy."

"I'm coming, Francine! Toby, I've got to get off the phone. Listen, thanks for calling."

"Any time."

CHAPTER 10

Diane Calls Mick

"Hello?"

"Hello, Mick? Do you know who this is?"

"Huh?"

"No? You'll have to guess."

"What?"

"I'll give you a hint. I have red hair."

"Wait. I—"

"Don't you want to guess?"

"No. Susan, give me a break."

"Susan? No, it isn't Susan. Try again."

"Come on, Susan. What are you giving me a hard time for? First you wake me up from a nap. Then—"

"Hey, wait a minute. Is this Mick?"

"What? Who?"

"Is this Mick?"

"No."

"Isn't this 555-4334?"

"No, it isn't."

"Oh. I have the wrong number."

"Yes, you do."

"Sorry."

Slam!

CHAPTER 11

Diane Calls Mick Again

"Hello?"

"Mick?"

"No. This is Mick's dad."

"Is Mick there?"

"I think so. He was getting ready to go to practice. Hold on. I'll see if he left."

"Hello?"

"Hello, Mick. How are you?"

"Hi. Sarah? What happened to your voice? You got a cold?"

"No, it isn't Sarah, Mick."

"I didn't think so. You sure have a sexy voice."

"Thanks. So do you."

"Who is this?"

"You have to guess."

"What?"

"Can't you guess?"

"Uh—let me think. Are you in McSwail's home-room?"

"No."

"I like that little giggle. I think I've heard it before. Do you have black hair?"

"No."

"You sure?"

"Sure, I'm sure."

"This isn't Rosanna?"

"No. Not even close."

"Hmmm . . ."

"I'll give you one hint. I have red hair. Sort of coppery."

"Yeah?"

"Can't you guess?"

"Hmmmm . . ."

"I'll give you one more hint. Someone I know is in your gym class."

"That's a hint?"

"Yes."

"That's not a hint."

"Yes, it is."

"Hmmmmm . . ."

"Someone I know is in your gym class, and you said something to him."

"Hmmmm . . ."

"Doesn't ring a bell?"

"No."

"Come on, Mick."

"Give me another hint."

"Someone I know is in your gym class, and you said something to him about me."

"It *is* Rosanna!"

40

"No, it's not."

"Oh."

"You don't remember?"

"No. I don't think so."

"It's Diane."

"Diane?"

"Diane Clarke."

"Huh? Do I know you?"

"Oh, God. Sorry."

Click!

CHAPTER 12

Diane Calls Mick

"Hi, Mick. I'm sorry I hung up like that."

"No, it's Mick's dad. I'll see if he's still here."

"Hello?"

"Hi, Mick. It's me again."

"Diane?"

"Yeah. I just wanted to say I'm sorry we got cut off like that."

"I thought maybe you hung up."

"Uh—no. My finger slipped."

"Oh."

"I didn't mean to cut you off. It was an accident."

"Yeah. I see. Well, it was nice of you to call back. I've got to go to practice."

"I know. I mean, your dad said you were getting ready to leave."

"Yeah. Coach doesn't like us to be late. If we're late, we do laps. Lots of laps."

"That's a downer."

"No, I don't mind. I kinda like doing laps. Keeps you in shape."

"Well, you're in great shape!"

"What?"

"I mean, I go to the games. You're really good."

"Yeah. Thanks."

"Well, I just wanted to apologize for hanging up—I mean, cutting us off like that."

"Yeah. Who are you again? You're not in McSwail's homeroom?"

"No, I'm a sophomore."

"Ha-ha! You don't sound like a sophomore."

"Is that a compliment?"

"Maybe. What's your last name?"

"Clarke. Diane Clarke. I'm Toby's sister."

"What? Oh, now I get it!"

"What do you mean?"

"I get it. You're Toby's sister. Toby put you up to this, right?"

"Well, yes. I mean, no. What do you mean?"

"Why is Toby on my case?"

"On your case?"

"Yeah."

"I don't know what—"

"Why is he doing this to me? I didn't do anything to him. I hardly even know him."

"Mick, I really don't think he's *doing* anything to you. He told me that—"

"Is this some sort of psych experiment, or something? Yeah. I'm right, aren't I? Your brother is such a brain. He's probably doing some kind of psych experiment. And I'm his guinea pig. You're recording this, aren't you! You're helping him, right? Where is he? Put him on."

"No. You're crazy! I don't know what you mean."

"Come on, Diane. I'm not as dumb as people think. I figured it out. Put Toby on. He's listening to this whole thing, right?"

"No, he isn't. He isn't even home. He's studying at a friend's."

"Studying new ways to torture me. Tell him I don't want to play."

"Well, gee whiz, Mick. I'm sorry if talking to me is what you call torture."

"What are *you* mad about? I didn't call *you*, did I? I didn't make *you* late for practice for some stupid psych experiment."

"I'm not a psych experiment!"

"Look, Diane—I'm late for practice."

"You really didn't say anything to Toby about me in gym class?"

"I'm going to say a lot to him next time I see him."

"But you didn't say anything about me?"

"Huh-uh. How could I? I don't know you."

"Maybe this is a psych experiment. And *I'm* the guinea pig."

"Ask your brother."

"I may murder him first."

"Well, he's *your* brother."

"Not really. My mother married his father. He came along as part of the package."

"Yeah. Look, I really don't have time to hear your family history, you know. I'm late."

"Okay, okay. So you're late. You don't have to be so nasty."

"Listen, have a nice life, okay? I've got to go. Really."

"Okay. I can take a hint."

"Come on, Diane. Don't go away mad. Just go away! Ha-ha-ha!"

Click.

CHAPTER 13

Toby Calls Julie

"Hello?"

"Hello, Julie? This is Toby."

"I'll go get her, Toby. This is her mom."

"Hello?"

"Hi, Julie. It's me."

"Hi. Did you do it? Did you get Diane to call Mick?"

"I don't know. I'm not calling about that. I called about my chemistry notes. I'm studying over at Zack's. I can bring them over to you later. Okay?"

"Yeah. Sure. Whatever. I don't care. I just care about Diane. Did you get her to call Mick Wilson?"

"Julie, I don't like the way you sound. This little joke we're playing on Diane means too much to you."

"No, it doesn't. Getting revenge is the most important thing in my life right now, but it doesn't mean too much."

"You're sick, Julie."

"Your sister is the sicko. She started the whole thing, remember?"

"Yes. But—"

"So what happened?"

"Look, I'm at Zack's. We're studying. I don't have time to—"

"Sure, you do. What happened? Did you tell her?"

"To call Mick? Yes."

"And did she?"

"I don't know. She wasn't home last night. She was at Francine's. And tonight I'm not home."

"So you don't know?"

"That's what I said. I don't know. I don't think she called last night, though. Listen, Julie, I feel terrible about doing this to her."

"Toby, it's too soon to feel terrible. Wait till she calls Mick and totally embarrasses herself and has to run away from home and change her identity forever! *Then* feel terrible."

"But she's going to kill me! You know, redheads have terrible tempers. It isn't just a stereotype. It's a true stereotype."

"Well, Toby, I didn't force you to do it. I didn't twist your arm."

"Diane's going to twist my arm. She's going to twist my neck! She's going to twist everything! I'm going to look like a human pretzel for the rest of my life!"

"Oh, lighten up. It'll be worth it, won't it?"

"Worth it? Have you truly gone nuts? How will it be worth it!"

"Stop shouting at me."

"You're right. I've got to cool it. I've got to calm down. I might be worrying for no reason. She probably won't even call Mick."

"Won't call him? What do you mean? She'd better call him!"

"Now *you* stop shouting, Julie. You tricked me into doing this. You hypnotized me or something."

"I couldn't hypnotize you. How could I hypnotize you? You have to have a brain to be hypnotized!"

"Oh, listen to her. She made a joke! Better go write that down in your diary. 'Made up my first joke today.'"

"You know, sarcasm is the lowest form of humor."

"Where'd you read that—in a Little Golden Book? Why don't you write that in your diary, too?"

"I don't keep a diary, Toby."

"Of course not. Your life is too boring even for you to write about."

"At least I go out on dates, Toby. I don't sit at home watching horror movies on the VCR every weekend of my life!"

"I watch horror movies because they remind me of you!"

"You watch horror movies because you're a social retard!"

"I *must* be a retard! I talk to you!"

"That's so juvenile!"

"Juvenile enough for you to understand?"

"You're just jealous of me because I'm popular."

"Popular? Popular? You weren't too popular with Mick Wilson, were you! Ha-ha!"

"Oh. That's low. That's low even for you."

"I know. But it's not too low for you! Ha-ha!"

"Stop laughing. Just shut up!"

"You shut up!"

"You shut up first. You're such a pig, Toby. Good-bye."

"Oink-oink."

"So when will you bring the chemistry notes over? About ten?"

"Yeah. Okay. About ten."

"See you later."

"Right. See you later."

═══ CHAPTER 14 ═══

Diane Calls Toby

═══

"Hello?"

"Hello, Zack?"

"No. Max, his brother."

"Little Max? Aren't you staying up awfully late?"

"I don't know. I can't tell time."

"Well, where are your mom and dad?"

"Gone somewhere. Zack's taking care of me."

"I see. Is Toby there?"

"Who?"

"Toby. Zack's friend."

"I guess."

"Well, could you go get him, please? Tell him it's Diane."

"I guess. *Hey, Toby! Toby! A girl wants to talk to you!*"

"Hello?"

"Max is wrong. I don't want to talk to you."

"Diane?"

"In fact, I may never talk to you again."

"Diane. Listen—"

"You're history, Toby."

"No, wait—"

"You're dead meat."

"That's no way for a sister to talk."

"Why, Toby? Why'd you do it?"

"Uh—I guess you called Mick, huh?"

"Why? Just tell me why."

"I guess you called Mick and it didn't go too well, huh?"

"Why, Toby? Why? Why? Why?"

"I guess it didn't go too well and now you're a little sore?"

"Why did you do that to me, Toby? I can only think of three possible reasons why you would do that to me."

"What are they?"

"Number one—you're sick."

"What's number two?"

"Number two is you're sick. And so is number three."

"I see."

"So which is it, Toby? One, two, or three?"

"None of the above, Diane. I'm sorry you're so upset."

"Upset? Why should I be upset? Because my own brother makes up a phony story and tricks me into calling the most popular boy in school and making a total fool of myself? Because by tomorrow everyone in school will know, and people will be laughing at me for the rest of my life?"

"Well—uh—I only did it for you, Diane."

"What? I think we have a bad connection, Toby. It sounded like you said you did it for me."

"I did. For you and Julie."

"Julie? What has she got to do with this?"

"It was her idea. I mean—I did it so you two could stop fighting and be friends again."

"Toby, not one word you're saying makes any sense. Hold on just for a second."

"Hold on? Why?"

"Because I'm going to scream."

"But, Diane—"

"Aaaaaaiiiiiiiiieeeeee!"

"Diane?"

"Okay. Where were we?"

"I was explaining about Julie."

"Well? What about Julie? The two of you cooked up this little scheme?"

"Yeah. I guess. But we—"

"But why? Why would she want to do this to me? And why would you go along with it?"

"She said if she got revenge against you, then the two of you could make up."

"Oh. Right. That makes perfect sense. Thanks for clearing it all up, Toby. Hold on just for a second, okay?"

"Hold on?"

"Aaaaaaiiiiiiiiieeeeee!"

"Diane, do you have to keep doing that?"

"Yes. Yes, I do. I really do. Go on."

"So, getting you to call Mick Wilson and embarrass yourself was Julie's revenge. Now you two can bury the hatchet."

"Sorry, Toby. It still isn't making any sense. Could you maybe explain *why* Julie had to have revenge against me, her oldest and dearest friend?"

"Yes. Yes, I can."

"Aaaaaaiiiiiiiiiieeeeeeeeyaaaaah! Go on, Toby."

"You don't know?"

"No, Toby. I don't."

"For telling her to call Mick Wilson and pretend to interview him for the school paper."

"What? What did you say?"

"You heard me, Diane. You told her to call Mick Wilson, and she—"

"Mick Wilson? No, I didn't."

"You didn't?"

"I told her to call Mick Hardesty. Carol Trager's brother said that Mick Hardesty liked Julie and wanted to ask her out. But you know how shy he is."

"Mick Hardesty?"

"Uh-huh."

"Not Mick Wilson?"

"Why would I tell her to call Mick Wilson? He doesn't know she's alive. He doesn't know I'm alive, either. At least, he didn't until I called him up and embarrassed myself for life!"

"Mick Hardesty?"

"Will you stop repeating that name over and over?"

"Yeah. Okay. Mick Hardesty?"

"So Julie called Mick Wilson, too, huh. That's why she's been acting so berserk. I couldn't figure it out."

"Yeah. That's why. It was all just a big misunderstanding."

"I tried to do something nice for her."

"Mick Hardesty?"

"What's wrong with Mick? He's an okay guy. He's a little quiet, but he's real nice."

"A little quiet! People are always lifting his eyelids to see if he's alive!"

"Stop it, Toby."

"Remember *Night of the Living Dead*? That was Mick Hardesty!"

"Stop. You're not funny."

"At least I'm breathing!"

"You sound positively jealous."

"Jealous? Of what?"

"You don't like the idea of Julie going out with Mick, do you?"

"Don't be stupid. I didn't say that. I just said that Mick Hardesty has about as much personality as vanilla yogurt. I didn't say—"

"You're jealous. For sure. If you like Julie so much, Toby, why don't you ask her out? You're already plotting with her against your own sister! Go ahead, ask the little traitor out!"

"Stop trying to change the subject, Diane. We're not talking about me. Look. You and Julie are even now. So you can make up and—"

"Even? Even? How do you figure we're even?"

"Well—"

"I tried to do something nice for her, and she played a vicious trick on me in return! Everyone will know by tomorrow. I'll never live this down!"

"But you—"

"You think we're even? I'll tell you when we'll be

even, Toby. We'll be even after I get my revenge! I'm going to pay her back for betraying our friendship and making a fool out of me when I was only trying to be nice. Then we'll be even!"

"But, Diane—"

Click.

═══ CHAPTER 15 ═══
Diane Calls Julie
───

"Hello?"

"Hello, Julie? This is Diane."

"No, this is Julie's dad. Julie's asleep. She went to bed over an hour ago. It's a little late to be calling, isn't it, Diane?"

"I don't know. I don't know what time it is. I don't know anything."

"Diane, you seem a little agitated. Is there anything I can—"

"Could you give Julie a message for me, Mr. Reynolds?"

"Certainly."

"Would you please tell her that our friendship is over forever, that I'm never speaking to her again as long as I live, and that I'll never forgive her for what she did to me, and that I'll get back at her if it's the last thing I ever do."

"Hold the line a minute, Diane. I'd better get a pencil and paper. I'm not sure I can remember all that."

"Well—"

"Okay. Now what was that again?"

"Oh, never mind. Just tell her that I'm mad enough to spit."

"Okay. Mad—enough—to— Did you say 'spit'?"

"Yes. Good night, Mr. Reynolds."

"Night, Diane."

CHAPTER 16

Jennifer Calls Toby

"Hello?"

"Hello, Toby?"

"No. This is Diane. Is that you, Julie? I can't believe you're calling me. Didn't you get my message?"

"No. This isn't Julie. Please stop shouting at me. Is Toby there?"

"Oh. Sorry. I thought you were someone else."

"I *am* someone else."

"Yes. I know. But I thought you were someone else else."

"Listen, it's been nice chatting with you, but is Toby there?"

"Yes, he's here. Just a minute. *Toby—phone for you!*"

"Hello?"

"Hello, Toby?"

"Hi. Julie?"

"No. It's not Julie."

"You're right. You don't sound like Julie. Who is it?"

"A secret admirer."

"Ha-ha! Really?"

"I like your laugh, Toby. It reminds me of someone on TV."

"Tom Selleck, maybe?"

"No. More like Pee-Wee Herman. Very sexy."

"You think Pee-Wee Herman is sexy?"

"I think men with a sense of humor are sexy. Don't you?"

"Well, I've never given much thought to men with a sense of humor. Now, come on, who is this?"

"I told you. A secret admirer."

"I don't think we should have secrets between us, do you? Ha-ha!"

"You're very funny. I really mean that."

"I love your voice. It's so soft and whispery. Aren't you going to tell me who you are?"

"It's Jennifer."

"Jennifer?"

"Jennifer Exley."

"*The* Jennifer Exley?"

"I hope there aren't two of us. Ha-ha!"

"I like your laugh, too. How's it going?"

"Fine. Just fine."

"Gee, that was too bad in chemistry this afternoon, Jennifer."

"I know. I sniffed the wrong test tube. It was awful. I thought I was going to die."

"So did everyone else, the way you were shrieking and holding your nose. Are you okay?"

"The doctor said I didn't do any permanent damage to my nose. I just burned off all my nasal hair."

"I can't believe I'm talking to Jennifer Exley about her nasal hair!"

"What? What did you say, Toby?"

"I said, gee, that's a terrible shame. I guess you have to keep off it for a while, huh?"

"Keep off my nose? Ha-ha! That's a joke, right."

"Yeah."

"You're so funny. I've been admiring you all semester in chemistry class. You're very smart."

"Well, chemistry isn't really my best subject. You should see me in remedial wood shop!"

"Oh, you're just being modest."

"I am?"

"You're so brilliant. You always know which test tubes you shouldn't sniff."

"I don't sniff *any* test tubes. That's my secret, Jennifer."

"Well, too bad you didn't tell me your secret this afternoon. Maybe I'd still have my nasal hair."

"Yeah. Too bad."

"Listen, Toby, do you think we could study together some time?"

"Do I think— Yes! Of course, we can. I mean, sure!"

"Oh, that would be very nice. Do you think maybe tomorrow night would be good? My parents will be away the whole night, and it will be very quiet around here."

"Your parents? Great! I mean, yes. That sounds very good for studying. I mean, the quiet part sounds good. For studying, of course."

"You're so funny. Will you come over about seven-thirty? We can have the whole evening to ourselves."

"I can be there *now* if you'd like to get a head start. Ha-ha!"

"Ha-ha! Please, Toby, don't make me laugh so much. It hurts my nose."

"I'm sorry."

"I'm glad you're coming over tomorrow. I'd really like to get to know you better."

"Uh—me, too. I mean— You know what I mean. Okay, Jennifer. See you tomorrow."

"Nighty-night, Toby. Sweet dreams."

"Don't worry!"

"What?"

"I said goodbye. See you tomorrow."

══════ CHAPTER 17 ══════

Toby Calls Julie

──────────

"Hello?"

"Hi, Julie. You won't believe who just called me!"

"I think Julie's asleep, Toby."

"Oh. Hi, Mrs. Reynolds. Sorry."

"I'll go see if she's awake."

"Thanks."

"Hello?"

"Julie?"

"Oh. It's you."

"You don't have to be so enthusiastic, you know."

"Give me a break. I was asleep."

"How could you tell?"

"Did you call me up to act stupid? Of course, you don't have to *act!*"

"No. Sorry. I–I'm not sure why I called, really. You wouldn't be interested in who called me."

"You're right. I wouldn't."

"Jennifer Exley."

"You're right. I wouldn't."

"Jennifer Exley called me. The foxiest girl in school!"

"Does she want you to mow her lawn?"

"No. She had a much more personal request."

"She wants you to baby-sit her dog?"

"Very funny, Julie. Great line. I'm impressed. You should go to sleep more often."

"I'd like to, but some nerd keeps waking me up to tell me about Jennifer Exley."

"Yeah. Jennifer Exley. She invited me over. Her parents are going to be away."

"Jennifer Exley is not interested in you."

"What? Get real! How can you say that?"

"Easy. Jennifer Exley is not interested in you. I can prove it."

"How?"

"You have no money, right?"

"Right."

"There. I proved it. Jennifer Exley is not interested in you."

"You're bananas, Julie. There are other things in the world besides money."

"Not to Jennifer Exley."

"There's brains. There's a sense of humor—"

"Not to Jennifer Exley."

"Stop saying that."

"Make me. I've been to her house, Toby. Her towels all have dollar signs monogrammed on them! Her old doll house from when she was a kid is bigger than your house. Her house is so big, it has different *wings!* Have you ever been in a wing of a house, Toby? Of course not. That's why she's not interested in you. You don't have wings. She's a rich snob, and she only hangs out with other rich snobs."

"You sound really jealous."

"Jealous of her big house? Don't be ridiculous."

"Jealous that she invited me over."

"I repeat. Don't be ridiculous. Why'd you call me? To make me jealous? No way. I'm not jealous. Have a great time. Send me a postcard from the east wing! She probably wants you to sweep it!"

"She wants me to study chemistry with her."

"She has servants to study chemistry with her! She doesn't need you. She's not interested in you, Toby. Trust me."

"Good night, Julie. Sorry I bothered you. I shouldn't have called so late."

"I didn't hurt your feelings, did I?"

"No. Not at all. Good night."

"Bye, Toby."

CHAPTER 18

Diane Calls Mick

"Hello?"

"Hello, Mick? This is Diane Clarke."

"This is Mick's dad. You girls just never stop calling him, do you!"

"No. I guess not."

"I'll see if he's here. *Hey, Mick! Mick!*"

"Hello?"

"Hi, Mick. It's Diane. Diane Clarke."

"Who?"

"Let's not go through that again. I'm Diane, Toby Clarke's sister."

"Oh. Yeah. The psych experiment."

"Right. I'm the psych experiment."

"What's going on? Toby tell you to call me again?"

"No. No, I'm calling on my own."

"Yeah?"

"Yeah. I mean, yes. Mick, could you do me a favor?"

"I don't know."

"It's about Julie."

"Who?"

"Julie. The girl who pretended to interview you for the school paper."

"Oh, yeah. Toby sent her over here, too, right?"

"Wrong. I did."

"You did?"

"But it was a mistake."

"I don't follow any of this."

"That's okay. I just need you to do me a favor. I want to play a little joke on Julie because these calls were all her fault."

"They were?"

"Yes."

"But I thought—"

"Is that foreign exchange student still living in your house?"

"You mean Water Buffalo? Yeah. We're stuck with him until June."

"Water Buffalo? I thought his name was Ramar?"

"Yeah, his name is Ramar. But I call him Water Buffalo. Want to know why?"

"I'll bite."

"Because he looks like one! Ha-ha-ha!"

"That's not very nice."

"I saw a picture of a water buffalo in my world geography text, and I said, 'Hey—it's Ramar!' I've been calling him that ever since. He doesn't know what it is. He thinks it's a compliment! Ha-ha! I told him it means 'handsome' in American. So he's been telling everyone to call him Water Buffalo. It's a riot, isn't it?"

"Yes. A riot."

"You think so? Actually, it's not that funny. He's eating us out of house and home. He eats bags and bags of peanuts every day and throws the shells on the floor. He says they're good for his complexion. You ever see his complexion? His face looks like the surface of the moon! And he never takes a bath. He sits in the living room most of the time, taking up almost the whole couch, and he plays the same song over and over on some kind of bagpipes."

"Weird."

"Tell me about it."

"What country does he come from?"

"It's an island kingdom somewhere off the coast of Norway. I think it's called the Isle of Chicken."

"Chicken?"

"He told me it was named after some ship captain who grounded his ship on it."

"Captain Chicken?"

"Yeah. I guess. Anyway, I'll bet they foreign exchanged him just to get him out for a year so they could clean up!"

"Well, here's what I was wondering, Mick. I was wondering if Ramar has a date for the homecoming dance after the basketball game in two weeks."

"Ha-ha-ha! Are you putting me on? Of course not! Ha-ha-ha-ha!"

"Stop laughing."

"I'm on the floor! Ha-ha-ha! You're hysterical! A date? Ramar out on a date? How could he? He'd have to share his peanuts! Ha-ha-ha!"

"Mick, please. Stop!"

"You want a date with Ramar? You're in love with his long, blond hair, right? Too bad it's down to his knees."

"No. I told you, I want to play a joke on Julie."

"You mean—"

"Julie doesn't have a date to the homecoming dance."

"And you want—"

"I want you to tell Ramar to call her and ask her out."

"But isn't this girl a friend of yours?"

"Yes. She's my best friend."

"You wouldn't do that to a friend, would you?"

"I might."

"Oh, man! That's baaad!"

"I owe her one."

"So what do I have to do?"

"It's simple. Just get Ramar to call Julie and ask her out."

"I don't know. The last time he picked up the phone receiver, he tried to eat it."

"Come on, Mick. He can't be that gross."

"I didn't tell you any of the gross parts."

"Tell him to ask her to the dance and not to take no for an answer."

"Don't worry. Ramar doesn't know the word *no*."

"Great. So you think you can get him to do it?"

"If I hold up a cheeseburger in front of his face, he'll do anything I tell him. Or I should say, a bag of cheeseburgers."

"And you'll do it for me?"

"Yeah. If you'll pay for the cheeseburgers."

"I'll pay. I'll pay. Thanks, Mick."

"I still think it's real mean."

"I know. It's just mean enough. The homecoming dance will be the most embarrassing, most humiliating night in Julie's life, right?"

"If she survives it. I just hope she doesn't dance with him. Ramar's got the wettest, clammiest hands I ever saw. It's like he's a sponge or something. There are these gooey, wet handprints all over my house. They stay on the furniture for days. She'll be sopping wet before the dance is over."

"Ooh, gross. That's terrific."

"Wow, I'm glad I don't have a best friend like you."

"Thanks, Mick."

"It's nothing. Why am I doing this for you?"

"Because it's a good joke?"

"No, that's not why."

"Because you'd like to see Ramar go out on a date?"

"No."

"Because I promise not to bother you again if you do this for me?"

"Yeah. You got it."

"Okay. I can take a hint. Bye, Mick."

"Bye, Diane."

═══ CHAPTER 19 ═══

Toby Calls Julie

───

"Hello?"

"Julie, did I wake you?"

"It's Julie's dad, Toby. You woke me. What time is it?"

"I'm not sure exactly."

"Hmmm—my clock says 2:06 A.M. Why are you calling at 2:06 A.M.?"

"Uh—I thought you might still be up. Sorry."

"Hello?"

"Julie, is that you? This idiot friend of yours called at 2:06. Oh. Now it's 2:07. Even later."

"Go back to sleep, Dad. I'll talk to him. Hi, Toby."

"How'd you know it was me?"

"Dad said *idiot,* didn't he?"

"He shouldn't have said that."

"Well, you know my dad's an English teacher. He always chooses his words very carefully."

"I mean, he shouldn't have said that after the night I've had."

"You had a bad night?"

"The worst night of my life. The most embarrassing night of my life. I can never leave the house again. I have to get my name changed and my face changed and move somewhere high in the Himalayas and live as a hermit in a cave with only mountain goats for companions."

"Well, getting your face changed isn't a bad idea."

"Thanks for the support, Julie."

"Did you call to tell me all the juicy details?"

"No. I called for some sympathy, but I guess I called the wrong person."

"Okay. I'll give you sympathy. I'll give you lots of sympathy—if you tell me all the juicy details first."

"Julie!"

"Start at the beginning. Don't leave anything out."

"No. Your attitude is all wrong. You're ready to enjoy this—and it was the most embarrassing, humiliating night of my life."

"I won't enjoy it, I promise. But how can I be sympathetic if I don't know what to be sympathetic about?"

"Okay. You're right. That makes sense, I guess. But stop smirking like that."

"How do you know I'm smirking? You can't see me over the phone."

"I can hear it in your voice. You smirk with your voice."

"Toby, it's 2:11 in the morning. Are you going to tell me this horror story or not?"

"Okay. Okay. It's painful, that's all. It's real painful. You promise you're going to be sympathetic?"

"Yes, yes. I promise. I promise!"

"Well—Jennifer Exley—"

"I told you so!"

"What? What did you just say?"

"I told you so!"

"I don't believe you, Julie! All I said was Jennifer Exley, and you—"

"I told you so!"

"How can you say that?"

"I told you so!"

"Is that your idea of sympathy?"

"No. But I *did* tell you so."

"You really are jealous, aren't you!"

"I am not jealous. I just told you so."

"I'm really sorry I called. I thought you were a friend. Bye."

"Toby?"

Click.

=== CHAPTER 20 ===
Julie Calls Toby

===

"Hello, Toby?"

"You have reached the Clarke residence. No one is here right now to receive your call. Please leave a message when you hear the beep, and we'll call you back as soon as we can."

Beeeep.

"Come on, Toby. I know you're home. Pick up the phone. Come on. I'm calling to apologize. I'm throwing myself at your feet to beg for forgiveness. The least you can do is pick up the phone. I know you're there."

"You're throwing yourself at my feet?"

"I *knew* you were home. You creep!"

"Creep? This is how you beg my forgiveness?"

"Well, we each have our own special ways."

"Julie, I'm really ticked off at you."

"I know. And you're right. I was terrible last night. I was half asleep, but you were absolutely right to get mad at me. I wasn't a very good friend. That's why I'm calling. To apologize. I'm really sorry. You were in pain and all I did was make fun of you. I feel awful about it, Toby. I really do. I hope you'll accept my apology."

"Well, okay. Let's just forget about last night. Wow. I wish I could forget about *all* of last night!"

"Why? What happened?"

"Well, Jennifer Exley—"

"I told you so!"

Click.

CHAPTER 21

Julie Calls Toby Back

"Hello?"

"I'm sorry."

"Yeah. You're real sorry, Julie."

"It was a joke. Have you lost your sense of humor entirely?"

"Yes, I have. I've lost all my self-respect, all my dignity, and my sense of humor."

"You never had any self-respect or dignity. That's why you needed a sense of humor!"

"I guess that's your idea of an apology."

"I'm just trying to make you laugh. I'm just trying to cheer you up."

"Forget it."

"Well, what happened last night? What was so horrible?"

"You really want to know?"

"Yes. Of course I want to know. I won't make any

more jokes, I promise. And I won't say I told you so. Even if it kills me."

"Well, I went over to Jennifer Exley's."

"Yes. Go on."

"I was waiting for you to say 'I told you so.'"

"I promised. I won't say it. Go on."

"Just testing."

"So you went over to Jennifer's house to study chemistry, right?"

"Right. She came on all sexy over the phone in this whispery voice, saying how her parents would be away for the whole night and how she wanted to get to know me better."

"So you ran over there like an eager puppy with your tail wagging and your tongue hanging out."

"Julie!"

"Sorry. It just slipped out. Go on."

"What a house! I've driven by it before, but I never realized how immense it is. It's a real mansion."

"I told you. It has wings."

"I walked up the drive but I didn't know which door to go to. There were so many of them, and they all looked like front doors! It was weird."

"Is *that* your embarrassing story? You couldn't figure out which was the front door?"

"Shut up, Julie."

"Okay."

"Anyway, Jennifer met me at one of the doors. She acted real glad to see me, like we were close friends or something. She was wearing this sexy sweater and these real tight jeans and—"

"You can skip the physical description. I already know what Jennifer looks like."

"Yeah. Right. So she took my arm and kinda snuggled against me and led me down this long hall to the den. It was a great den. All these dark panelled walls and soft leather couches, and a big, warm fire going in this amazing fireplace."

"Sounds real romantic."

"I'm ignoring your sarcasm. I sat down on the couch in front of the fire, and she sat down real close to me and kept smiling at me, these real warm, meaningful smiles. And she kept saying how she's wanted to get to know me better and how she's wanted to invite me over for months and months. I couldn't believe it!"

"I'll bet."

"What's that supposed to mean?"

"Nothing. Nothing at all. I was just being sympathetic. Go on."

"Well, I got out my chemistry notes. But she said there was plenty of time for that later. She told me to get comfortable, to take off my shoes. So I did. Then she told me to stretch out on the couch and make myself at home. Then she started to unbutton my shirt."

"She *what?*"

"She unbuttoned my shirt. She said it was too warm in the den and I'd be more comfortable that way. Then she got up and said not to move, that she would be right back with a nice surprise for me."

"A surprise?"

"Yes. A *nice* surprise. Then she gave me this real sexy, meaningful grin, and left the room. I was in shock. I was in heaven! I was ready to float to the ceiling."

"Don't get disgusting."

"I just lay there on the couch, imagining what the nice surprise was going to be."

"And what was it?"

"Wait. Wait. What it was was a *disaster*. You're not going to believe this."

"I'm not going to live long enough to believe it! Will you go on?"

"So I'm lying there on the couch in front of the fire with my shoes off, just gazing into the fire, feeling real warm and cozy, waiting for Jennifer to return. I don't know how much time went by. Maybe five minutes, ten minutes. I don't know. I guess I was in this dreamlike state."

"Barf."

"I hear someone come in, so I look up from the fire. And it's Jennifer's dad!"

"He was home?"

"Yes, he was home. And he wasn't expecting anyone else to be in his home. And he certainly wasn't expecting anyone to be lying on the den couch with his shoes off and his shirt unbuttoned. He was in his underwear. And when he saw me lying on his couch, he jumped almost up to the chandelier and turned bright red."

"That's how you could tell he was surprised to see you?"

"Right. He's a real big guy, built like a bear. It took him a while to be able to speak, but then he started sputtering out questions. You know, 'Who are you? What are you doing here?'"

"Good lord."

"Well, I sat up real quick and smiled at him. I tried

to look like I didn't notice that he was in his underwear. I mean, I tried to be real casual. But it wasn't easy because I was real surprised to see him, too. And I said, 'I'm with Jennifer.' "

"And what did he say?"

"He said, 'No, you're not.' "

"What?"

"I told him I came over to study with Jennifer. And he said, 'That's impossible. Jennifer isn't home.' And I said, 'What do you mean? Of course she's home.' And he said, 'She isn't home. She left more than ten minutes ago. I saw her go out the door and get into her car. She had a date with Mick Wilson. She went over to Mick's house.' "

"You mean—"

"That's right. She left me there. It was all a setup, a joke. She knew her parents would find me sooner or later and throw me out."

"I don't believe it!"

"I told you you wouldn't."

"So what did you do?"

"What could I do? I put on my shoes. I buttoned my shirt."

"He was standing there the whole time?"

"That's right. In his underwear. Staring at me as if I was some kind of intruder or something, making sure I didn't steal an ashtray or a paperweight off the desk."

"How humiliating."

"Tell me about it."

"Didn't you just want to die?"

"Well—yes. I guess I was even more embarrassed than disappointed. I just felt totally humiliated in every way. Not because Jennifer's dad had caught me lying there on his couch like an idiot. But because Jennifer, a girl I didn't even know, had played such a mean trick on me."

"Mick put her up to it."

"I guess—"

"Well, I'm really sorry, Toby."

"Thanks."

"It was a rotten, low thing to do to you."

"Yes, it was."

"I can really understand how you must feel."

"Thanks."

"But I told you so!"

CHAPTER 22
Toby Calls Mick

"Hello?"

"Hello, Mick?"

"No. This is his mother. I'll get him for you."

"Hello?"

"Mick?"

"Yeah."

"It's Toby."

"Ha-ha-ha."

"I know why you're laughing, Mick."

"Yeah?"

"I just don't know why you did it to me."

"For a joke, man."

"A joke?"

"Yeah."

"I've never been so embarrassed in my life."

"I heard. Ha-ha."

"You heard?"

"Yeah. From Jennifer's dad."

"He told you about it?"

"We told him about the joke. He laughed so hard, he choked."

"You were all laughing, huh?"

"Yeah. We all had a good laugh."

"At my expense."

"Yeah."

"But, why?"

"I don't know."

"Come on, Mick. Why'd you do it to me?"

"For laughs. You know. Same reason you had those girls call me."

"Now, hold on a minute—"

"That girl who came over without any tape in her tape player and pretended to interview me?"

"I didn't tell her to do that."

"She said you did."

"That was all a misunderstanding."

"A misunderstanding, huh? What about your sister? You told her to call me, didn't you?"

"Well, yes. But that wasn't a joke on you. It was a joke on her."

"Very funny. I don't get it."

"It's kind of hard to explain."

"That's okay."

"But I still don't see why you had to play such a dirty trick on me."

"It wasn't a trick. It was just a misunderstanding. Ha-ha-ha!"

"You're a riot, Mick."

"Yeah. I know."

"So now we're even?"

"Yeah. Right, Tobe. Now we're even."

"Well, glad I could give you a few laughs."

"A few? Don't say a *few*, Tobe. We were hysterical for hours. I thought I'd bust a gut."

"Thanks, Mick. That's great. Very colorful way of putting it, too."

"But we're even now. No hard feelings, right?"

"What can I say? No hard feelings."

"Now I just have a little favor to do for your sister."

"My sister? What?"

"Uh—I guess that's between her and me."

"Oh, boy."

"I saw your sister in the lunchroom this afternoon. She's kind of cute."

"Yeah. I guess."

"She doesn't look like you at all. Guess that's why she's cute. Ha-ha-ha!"

"Yeah. Well, I think I've taken enough abuse for one lifetime. I'm going to say goodbye now, Mick."

"Don't think it hasn't been fun, because it hasn't! Ha-ha-ha!"

"Good one, Mick. Another good one. You've got a million of 'em, huh?"

"I don't know."

"Well, okay. See you around."

"Not if I see you first. Ha-ha-ha!"

"Right."

"Oh, hey, wait—Toby."

"Yes?"

"About those chemistry notes. Remember? Think I could borrow them tomorrow night?"

"Uh—sure. No problem."

"Great. Thanks a lot, Tobe. Later."

"Later, Mick."

CHAPTER 23

Ramar Calls Julie

"Hello?"

"Greetings. Do I have the pleasure of addressing the unmarried Julie Reynolds?"

"No. This is Julie's mother. Is she in some kind of trouble?"

"Trouble? I do not know the meaning of trouble."

"Oh. I—er—you sounded so formal and serious, I thought maybe—"

"You are Julie Reynolds's progenitor?"

"You're putting me on—right? Toby, is this you?"

"No. I am not understanding. As they say in my country, the dog flies when the wind blows hard enough. Is that a favorite expression of yours, too?"

"Well, no. Not exactly. Hold on a minute. *Julie! Julie! I think it's for you!*"

"Hello?"

"Do I have the gracious pleasure of addressing Julie in the flesh?"

"What? Fresh?"

"Fresh? No. Flesh."

"Julie Flesh? I think you have the wrong number."

"I have the unlucky number?"

"No. The wrong number. The wrong phone number."

"You will give me another number?"

"Who *is* this?"

"Is this Julie Reynolds in the flesh?"

"No. It's— I mean, yes! This is Julie Reynolds. Who is this?"

"I was previously in conversation with your antecedent."

"My aunt? No. That was my mom. Who *is* this?"

"I am speaking as your humble servant Ramar."

"Toby, you're not funny."

"Is that a witticism?"

"Toby, stop it! That's the phoniest foreign accent I ever heard!"

"The American sense of humor escapes me, I am afraid. We have an expression in my country—the fish don't bark alone. It always gives me a giggle. Are you familiar with it perhaps?"

"Toby, I'm losing patience."

"I am unfamiliar with this word *Toby*. Is it a form of greeting? If so, Toby to you, too, my flower."

"Toby—wait a minute. Did you say Ramar?"

"I can say it if it pleases you. Ramar."

"Is this really Ramar?"

"The same."

"Oh, good lord. Hi, Ramar. This is Julie."

"This is not a recording and I must hold myself in until the beep?"

"Ha-ha-ha!"

"Your laughter is the sound of crows."

"Gee, thanks. Is that a compliment in your country?"

"It is meant to be so. But it is hard to tell. We have no crows in my country. The birds fly south every winter and refuse to return the next spring."

"That's too bad. Listen, I'm kind of busy, Ramar."

"Busy as the two-legged horse?"

"Right."

"Then shall I keep my comments brief?"

"Yes. Please."

"Are you familiar with the words *cogent* and *terse?*"

"No. Not really."

"Neither am I."

"Ramar, please—"

"Julie, may I ask when you last visited my country? Was it in the winter? In the winter, the ponds freeze and we skate barefoot across the ice. I am sorry to report it is a custom that is dying out."

"Gee, I wonder why. Listen, I really have to go now."

"You are making the jest with Ramar?"

"What? Making what?"

"Your humor is swift and sharp like the knife that beheads the ox."

"Thanks. I guess. Well, bye. I've got to—"

"Shall I wait for the beep?"

"What?"

"My mouth reaches out to you, but I have not mastered the art of the telephone. In my country, the phones are silent because we all speak in sign language whenever possible. It's such good exercise."

"That's very interesting, Ramar. I'm really glad to know all these things about your country, but I really have to get off the phone now. Can you understand that?"

"I can understand when the ancients say enough is not nearly enough and too much is even less."

"See you at school—okay?"

"At the school dance, yes?"

"Yes. What?"

"Your answer has filled me with the joy of a newborn toad."

"What? I what?"

"By choosing to attend the dance with me, you have enlarged my heart."

"Your heart? Wait a minute, Ramar. I haven't— I mean—I— What dance?"

"I can hear the joy echoing in your voice like the sound of a million goldfish."

"No, Ramar. That's not joy. It's panic. What do you think I just agreed to?"

"The homecoming dance will be a night of a thousand memories burned into my chest like a bad tattoo."

"The homecoming dance? Wait a minute! Hold your horses!"

"My horses are unbridled, their saddle sores forgotten."

"Ramar, please! Stop with the colorful expressions!

I did *not* say I would go to the homecoming dance with you."

"When you said yes, you blew off the top of my head. Do you see, I have learned American expressions, too."

"Ramar—"

"If you describe the sarong you will be wearing, I will make certain that my kilt matches in color and fabric."

"My what? My sarong? No, Ramar. No. Please listen to me. I did not say yes. I am not going to that dance with you. I-I'd really like to. But—uh—I'm busy that night."

"Did you say that you would really like to? Well, do not have fear. I shall not disappoint. I will appear to accompany you at least two hours before the dance so you will not have time to worry about my arrival."

"No. Oh, no. What am I going to do?"

"Do you like peanuts?"

"Ramar, how can I get through to you? I did not say yes. I cannot go with you."

"Do you like them shelled or unshelled? My preference is for the unshelled. Sometimes you find one nut in the shell, and sometimes two. It is one of nature's mysteries, is it not? Our scientists have puzzled over the matter for years."

"Are we talking about nuts now? Ramar, I'm trying to be nice, but I've got to make you understand that I am not going to the dance with you. I just can't. I'm sorry."

"You do not need to try to be nice. Your essence is nice. I will observe the ritual cleansing procedures now to prepare for our date. I can promise only that our night will live on in my heart and will burn in my mind like a smoked tongue on an open pit barbecue. Until then, goodbye, my flower."

Click.

"No! Ramar—wait! I can't! Ramar! No!"

═══ CHAPTER 24 ═══
Julie Calls Ramar Back

───────

"Hello, Ramar. Listen, I can't—"

"Hey, sorry. Ramar just went out."

"What? He—who is this? Mick?"

"Yeah."

"This is Julie Reynolds. I was just talking to him, and he—"

"Oh, yeah? Was that you he was talking to on the phone? Wow, Julie. Whatever you said to him sure made him happy. He tossed his bag of peanuts up in the air and tore out of the house like an elephant on a stampede."

"Mick, listen. You've got to help me."

"Hey, I can see him out the window. He just ran headfirst into the mailbox on the corner."

"Mick, please—"

"Now he's backing up and doing it again. He's ramming his head into the mailbox. What did you say to him?"

"It's all a mix-up. He thinks I'm going to the homecoming dance with him."

"Yeah? You are? Wow. That's really nice of you, you know, to sacrifice your evening like that."

"No, I didn't—"

"No wonder the big guy is so happy. Look at him ramming his head out there. He's never had a date in his life. I don't think any girl ever talked to him before!"

"No, Mick. This can't be happening! You've got to help me get through to him."

"You're a really good person, Julie. Kids at school are going to tease you like crazy, but you don't even care, do you! That's great."

"No. I do care. I *do* care! Listen, Mick—"

"Did he offer to share his peanuts with you?"

"Yes, but—"

"Wow. The big guy has really fallen for you."

"Mick—stop! You've got to listen to me."

"Just one thing. Remember not to touch his hands if you can help it. They're always sopping wet and cold as ice. And don't say anything about his weight. He's very sensitive about his stomach bouncing up and down when he walks. So be careful not to stare at it or anything."

"I'm not going to stare at his stomach. Because I'm not—"

"That's good. I just thought I should warn you. If he has to turn sideways to squeeze through a doorway, just turn your head. Look the other way. That way he won't think you're staring at him. You'll have a good time. He's got a great sense of humor, I think. It's a really nice thing you're doing, Julie. When you came over to interview me that night, I thought you were weird. But I guess you're okay."

"Thanks, Mick. But—"

"I'm late for practice. See you around."

Click.

"Mick? Mick? Please, Mick. You've got to help get me out of this."

CHAPTER 25

Julie Calls Toby

"Hello?"

"Hello, Toby?"

"No. It's Diane. Julie, don't speak to me. I'm still not speaking to you."

"I'm not speaking to you. I'm calling Toby."

"Did you get my message?"

"What message?"

"Don't ask me questions. I told you I'm not speaking to you."

"Diane, is Toby home?"

"You and Toby have sure gotten chummy. Hope you two have been having a great time plotting against me."

"Diane—"

"Stop talking to me. I told you. You're not my friend. I guess you never were. I can't believe you played that rotten trick on me."

"But, Diane, you started it—"

"Stop talking, Julie. I'm not talking to you. I'm not talking to Toby, either. You're both nonpersons."

"Nonpersons? Diane—"

"I don't hear you. You're invisible. You're history. You're a nonperson. *Toby! Toby! Phone for you! Another nonperson!*"

"Hello?"

"Hi, Toby. It's me."

"Oh. Hi, Julie."

"Diane's still pretty mad."

"You picked up on that, huh? Yeah, she's mad all right."

"I've got other problems now. Even bigger problems."

"You sound pretty down. You know, I was so upset about Jennifer Exley, I forgot to tell you something yesterday. Something Diane told me."

"What?"

"It's about when she told you to call Mick, which started this whole fight between you two."

"Yes. What about Mick?"

"Well, Diane meant for you to call Mick Hardesty."

"Mick Hardesty?"

"Right."

"Not Mick Wilson? She didn't tell me to call Mick Wilson?"

"No. Mick Hardesty wanted you to call him, but you know how shy he is."

"I don't believe it."

"You don't believe he's shy?"

"I don't believe I called the wrong Mick."

"Well, that's what happened."

"I don't believe it."

"It was all just a mix-up."

"Just a mix-up. Just a mix-up! This little mix-up made me embarrass myself for life in front of Mick Wilson. It made me play a terrible trick on my best friend, who's no longer speaking to me and says I'm a nonperson! And you say it was just a mix-up?"

"Well—"

"No wonder Diane thinks I'm a terrible person. I *am* a terrible person! She was doing me a favor. And what did I do? Played a rotten trick on her in return!"

"But it was just a mix-up."

"Will you stop saying that?"

"Okay, okay. This isn't my fault, you know."

"Of course it's your fault. It's got to be your fault!"

"Will you chill out? How can it be my fault?"

"I don't know. But somehow you're to blame. I know it. I know you are. You're the one who tricked Diane into calling Mick Wilson, after all."

"Julie, you *made* me do that! It wasn't my idea—it was yours!"

"So what? You're supposed to be smart, Toby. You're not supposed to go along with every stupid idea I have."

"Well, excuse me for living. I'll never listen to anything you have to say again, okay? Why are you in such a bad mood, anyway?"

"I don't want to talk about it."

"Come on, Julie."

"No. Really. I don't want to talk about it. It's too depressing."

"It can't be that bad."

"Yes, it can. How do you know how bad it can be?"

"Well, whatever it is, it can't be as bad as you sound."

"Give me a break, Toby. At least I don't sound as bad as you look!"

"Ha-ha. Very funny. Is that going to cheer you up? To make dumb cracks about me?"

"Probably. A little."

"Well, no way. I'm hanging up."

"No. Don't hang up, Toby. I'm sorry. I'm just in a bad mood."

"You're not going to cry now, are you?"

"No. You'd enjoy it too much. I'm just all confused now. What should I do?"

"About what?"

"About Diane."

"Apologize to her, I guess."

"Apologize? How can I apologize?"

"By saying you're sorry. That's the normal way. Tell her you're sorry you played that vicious, humiliating trick on her after she was just trying to fix you up with Mick Hardesty."

"But how can I? She won't talk to me. She says I'm a nonperson. She called me that, right to my face."

"Okay, okay. I'll talk to her. I'll tell her you want to apologize."

"You're a nonperson, too."

"I'm a brother nonperson. That's different. Don't worry. I'll tell her."

"Thanks, Toby. That's very nice of you."

"Try to cheer up, okay? I don't like hearing you sound so low."

"Okay. I'll try. Thanks. Bye."

"Bye, Julie. I'll call you later."

CHAPTER 26

Mick Calls Diane

"Hello?"

"Hello, Diane? This is Mick."

"No. This is Diane's mother. Hold on. I'll see if she's home. *Diane! Diane!*"

"Hello?"

"Hi."

"Hi. Who is this?"

"It's me. Mick."

"What?"

"It's me. Mick Wilson. You know."

"Oh. Sorry, Mick. I was just surprised. I mean—"

"So? How's it goin'?"

"Uh—fine. Just fine."

"I was just wondering—I mean—I saw you in the lunchroom a few days ago, and—well—"

"Really? I didn't see you."

"Oh. Well, what I was calling about was—I thought

maybe you'd like to go with me to the homecoming dance after the game with Westerville."

"What? Hey—who *is* this?"

"I told you. Mick Wilson."

"And you're asking me out? Sure. I really believe that!"

"Whoa. Hold on—"

"What's the gag, Mick? Who told you to call me?"

"Nobody. I—"

"Did Julie tell you to call? Who was it?"

"Now, listen—"

"No way I'm falling for this one, Mick. You tell Julie or Toby or whoever it was I think you're all really juvenile!"

Slam.

CHAPTER 27

Julie Calls Diane

"Hello?"

"Hi, Diane. It's me. Please don't hang up."

"What?"

"Did Toby talk to you? Well, it doesn't really matter. I'm calling to apologize. I'm really sorry. The whole thing was a terrible mix-up, and I'll understand if you never want to speak to me again. But I just wanted you to know what happened, I mean about the mix-up. I just misunderstood you, you see. I thought you were telling me that Mick Wilson wanted me to call him. But of course you meant Mick Hardesty. But I didn't know that. So when I went over to Mick Wilson's and made such a fool of myself, I thought you had played a trick on me. That was my first mistake. Or maybe it was my second. But it was just a mistake, see. And I know I shouldn't have been angry at you because you were just trying to do me a favor, and the whole misunderstanding was my fault. But I got angry and then I got Toby to tell you that Mick Wilson wanted you to call him, just to get back at you. Poor Toby thought he was helping to patch things up between us. But of course he was just making things worse, and so was I because I was angry and didn't understand that it was all just a big misunderstanding on my part. Whew! I know I'm talking a mile a minute, Diane, but I just had to get it all out and explain to you and beg you to accept my apology."

"Who were you trying to reach?"

"What? Diane?"

"I'm sorry. There's no Diane here. You have the wrong number."

"Isn't this 555-9956?"

"No, it isn't."

"Oh. Sorry."

"You sound like a nice girl. I hope you work things out."

"Thanks a lot. Bye."

"Bye."

CHAPTER 28

Julie Calls Diane Again

"Hello?"

"Hello, Diane?"

"No. It's her mom. Is this Julie?"

"Yes, it is, Mrs. Clarke."

"What on earth is going on between you two, Julie?"

"I'm not sure exactly. It's all just a misunderstanding."

"Well, I do hope you two can settle it. Diane has been impossible for the past two weeks. She's been absolutely wired for sound!"

"I'm sure we can settle it. I just need to talk to her."

"Well, I'll see if she'll come to the phone. Really, Julie, it's none of my business, but this is just so childish."

"You're right."

"I'm right that it's none of my business?"

"No. That's not what I meant. I meant that you're right. It's childish."

"I had a best friend once, and we had a silly argument. I don't even remember what it was about. I think it had something to do with a dress. Or was it a boy? Oh, I guess you probably don't want to hear this."

"Probably."

"I'll get Diane. You sound as bad as she does. Hold the line."

"Okay. Thanks."

"Hello?"

"Diane?"

"Oh. It's you."

"Did Toby talk to you?"

"Yes. One nonperson standing up for another."

"Please, Diane. I just want to apologize."

"Okay. Go ahead. Don't forget to beg my forgiveness. Try to sound as pitiful as possible."

"Gee, you sure are making this easy for me."

"I'm giving you a chance, Julie. Only because we used to be good friends. But you played a mean trick on me. For no reason."

"I know. You're right."

"Is that it? Keep going."

"I'm really sorry. It was a mix-up. I thought you meant the wrong Mick."

"Toby told me."

"I shouldn't have gotten angry."

"I know."

"I shouldn't have played that trick on you."

"I know."

"That's why I'm calling to apologize. I want us to be

friends again, the way it was. No tricks, no jokes. No yelling. I admit it was my fault."

"Well, that's a start."

"A start?"

"We're not exactly even yet, are we?"

"Even? What do you mean?"

"Well, you haven't stopped playing tricks on me, have you?"

"Diane, I don't know what you mean."

"Get real, Julie. I'm not as dumb as you look."

"Hey, come on, Diane. I'm trying to apologize. I don't know what you're—"

"So I'm not going to fall for your latest gag. You tried it once too often."

"What latest gag, Diane? I really don't know what you're talking about."

"Well, here are two words that might remind you— *Mick Wilson.*"

"Huh?"

"Oh. I suppose you're going to pretend that you didn't tell Mick Wilson to call me and ask me to the homecoming dance."

"Huh?"

"You heard me."

"I haven't spoken a word to Mick Wilson since that horrible night at his house when I had no tape in my tape recorder, thanks to you."

"I don't believe you. Mick called tonight and—"

"Really? Well, I haven't spoken to him. I'm still too embarrassed. If I see him coming down the hall, I run the other way. I couldn't call him, Diane. No way I could ever call him."

"Oh good grief! That call was for real!"

"What?"

"He called and asked me to the dance. And I—I—"

"You thought it was a joke?"

"Right. And I told him off and hung up on him. Aaaaaayye!"

"Diane, what's that loud noise?"

"It's just me."

"What are you doing?"

"Pounding my head against the wall. Ouch!"

"Stop. Come on. Stop it. It sounds terrible."

"Ow. I hung up on him. Do you believe it? I hung up on Mick Wilson."

"Bad move, Diane. But you can't blame me for this one."

"Of *course* I blame you! If you hadn't played a trick on me in the first place, I never would've thought the real call was a trick, too! I would've known the real call was real!"

"But wait—"

"This is all your fault, Julie! Don't try to worm out of it!"

"You're not making any sense. Why would I play *two* tricks on you, Diane? Why would I do that?"

"Of course you had good reason to play another trick on me! Because of Ramar!"

"Ramar?"

"Because I sicced Ramar on you!"

"You? You?"

"Yes. I had to pay you back for your trick, didn't I?"

"So you got Ramar to ask me to the dance?"

"Yes. Pretty good trick, huh?"

"Good trick? Not only will I have the most miserable night of my life, but I'll be a laughingstock in front of the whole school!"

"You won't be a laughingstock. Everyone will just feel sorry for you. Ha-ha!"

"But—but how could you do that to me? I'm your best friend!"

"I was just getting even."

"But Ramar?"

"I was just getting even—plus a little more."

"That is the sneakiest, lowest, most disgusting, most disgraceful, most despicable thing one friend ever did to another friend!"

"Yeah. Probably."

"Bye, Diane. Don't ever speak to me again."

"Hey, what about your apology?"

Slam.

CHAPTER 29

Diane Calls Mick

"Hello, please?"

"Hello—Mick?"

"This is Mick?"

"No. I'm calling Mick."

"You are called Mick? That is a bizarre coincidence. There is also a youth named Mick who abides in this house."

"No, no. Ramar? Is this Ramar?"

"You are calling my name?"

"This is Diane Clarke. I am trying to reach Mick."

"You are reaching Ramar. Your tongue is in my ear, so to speak. Ha-ha! Do you enjoy my witticism?"

"Yes. Ha-ha. That's a riot. Is Mick—"

"Perhaps you would enjoy a peculiarly humorous anecdote that is told in my country."

"Perhaps I would. But not right now."

"That's okay. I am not remembering it too well,

anyway. It involves two armadillos and a pith helmet. Are you familiar with it?"

"No. No, I'm not."

"What a pity. It is quite daring, as I recall, and just a little bit naughty. Hee-hee."

"Maybe some other time, okay? Is Mick there?"

"Mick lives here. You are correct in that assumption."

"Ramar, is Mick there *now?*"

"As we say in my country, an empty dog sheds no light."

"What?"

"I guess it does not translate."

"I guess not."

"I am enjoying your voice in my head. Your voice is soft, like a girl's."

"That's probably because I'm a girl."

"You? A girl? Named Mick? I am filled with bewilderment."

"No. I am a girl named Diane."

"No wonder."

"No wonder what?"

"I do not know. I am a lowly seeker of answers, as are we all. The questions are many and the answers are few. As the wise men often say in my country, a healthy tree knows as many questions as a sick monkey."

"Ramar, I really must speak to Mick now. It's very important. He called me about the homecoming dance and—"

"The dance. Ah, my goodness yes. The dance. Thank you for your kind and gracious invitation. I most humbly accept."

"You what? No, wait—"

"We will be like the head and tail of a worm, moving as one wherever our heart bids us to slither and crawl."

"That's beautiful, Ramar. But you don't understand—"

"It is written in the book of time. I will escort you on wings of song."

"What does that mean?"

"It has no meaning. It is an expression."

"Ramar, I can't—I mean, you can't—I mean—"

"Thank you for asking me to the dance. I am overcome with pleasure and anticipation. My knees are trembling. My kidneys ache."

"No! No! Do you hear me? No!"

"Do you like peanuts?"

"No! No! No!"

"I will arrive two hours early so as not to keep you in suspense. I will gladly pay for my own ticket of admission, even though it was you who invited me to attend."

"No! No! No! Can't you hear me? No!"

"Okay. I will accede to your wishes. You may pay for my admission, too."

"No, please. Listen to me. You've got to listen to me!"

"I will listen as the mountain goat listens to the tin can in the grass. And until we meet, my tongue will be clucking your name."

"No, please. Please don't cluck my name. I'm begging you, Ramar. Don't cluck my name."

"You are making a witticism, right? I enjoy a

well-phrased witticism, even if I do not understand it. Hee-hee!"

"Uccch. That giggle. I'm going to be sick."

"I am sick with anticipation as well, my flower. Until we meet, until I am dazzled by the light of your golden aura, and dizzied by the thundering beauty of your feet moving across the dance floor, I will say good night."

Click.

"Ramar? Ramar? Is Mick there? Ramar?"

CHAPTER 30

Toby Calls Julie

"Hello?"

"Hello, Mrs. Reynolds?"

"No. It's Julie."

"Oh. Hi, Julie. You sounded like your mother."

"I don't know if that's a compliment or not."

"What are you doing?"

"Oh, nothing. Just staring."

"Staring? At what?"

"Nothing. Just staring."

"Julie, that isn't good. You should get some exercise."

"I do."

"What kind of exercise?"

"I sigh a lot."

"Oh, boy. Did you talk to Diane?"

"Yes."

"How'd it go?"

"Haven't you talked to her?"

"No. She still isn't talking to me. She just mopes around. And does a lot of staring. Staring seems to be very popular these days."

"You should try it."

"No thanks. I guess your apology didn't go over with her."

"You guess right."

"You're still not speaking to each other?"

"No. We're not speaking to each other *again.*"

"Bummer."

"Tell me about it."

"I called to cheer you up."

"You're doing a fab job."

"You know, being sarcastic doesn't help anyone."

"Right."

"There you go again."

"I can't help it. This is my new personality. No one ever thought I had a serious side, but I think I've found it. I'm going to stay serious for the rest of my life."

"Serious? You're not serious—you're morbid!"

"Maybe."

"Now you're getting *me* depressed."

"Tough."

"Listen, I—uh—called for another reason."

"Shoot."

"Well, I'm a little reluctant to ask you this. I think you're going to laugh at me."

"I'm never going to laugh again. I told you, Toby, I'm serious now."

"You promise you won't laugh?"

"Yes. I promise. I won't laugh. Try me. You'll see."

"Well, maybe this is a bad time to ask."

"Yes. It's a bad time. So ask anyway."

"Well—I know this is going to strike you funny, but I'm serious. I mean, it's not a put-on or anything."

"The suspense is killing me."

"I just wondered if—maybe—you'd like to go to the homecoming dance with me."

".........."

"Julie? Are you still there?"

".........."

"You're laughing, aren't you! That's not very nice."

"I'm not laughing. Really. I'm just surprised. You really surprised me."

"Well? Do you want to? It wasn't easy for me to ask, you know. I was sure you'd laugh at me."

"Yes. I'd like to, Toby. I really would. But I can't."

"Can't? What do you mean?"

"You haven't talked to Diane at all, huh?"

"No."

"Well—I already have a date."

"Oh, yeah? With who?"

"With—Ramar."

"Huh?"

"You heard me. With Ramar."

"Ha-ha-ha-ha! Stop, Julie. Don't make me laugh. I have chapped lips. Ha-ha-ha!"

"You're not going to have any *teeth* if you don't stop laughing."

"You're serious?"

"I told you, Toby. I'm going to be serious for the rest of my life. And now you know why."

"Ha-ha-ha! You and Ramar! I love it!"

"Stop laughing. I mean it. Stop laughing!"

"I'm sorry. Ha-ha! I don't think I can stop."

"It's not funny. I'm going to have to leave the country to get out of this date. I'm going to have to become an emigrant and go somewhere far away. Do you know how serious that is, giving up my American citizenship? Having to learn a whole new language, and wear clothes that don't fit, and eat cheese three times a day? That's what I'm going to have to do. So why are you laughing?"

"Did Ramar call you? Did he ask you out?"

"Yes."

"So why did you say yes? Did he threaten to sit on you, or something?"

"I didn't say yes, stupid. I said no."

"Oh. I get it. You said no, so that means you're going with him."

"I said no and I said no and I said no. I said it till I was blue in the face. But he didn't hear me. Or he didn't understand me. I don't know. I couldn't make heads or tails of anything he said. He kept talking about two-legged horses and skating barefoot."

"Makes perfect sense to *me!*"

"Then *you* go to the dance with him!"

"Sorry. He's not my type. I usually only go out with members of my own species! Ha-ha-ha!"

"You usually don't go out. Period."

"So?"

"Sew buttons."

"Is that your idea of wit?"

"I don't need wit. I'm talking to *you.*"

"Wait. Stop. Stop. I don't want to fight with you."

"I don't want to fight with you, either. I'm too miserable to fight with anyone."

"Well, you have to look at it this way. It's just one

date. It isn't the end of the world. What am I saying? Forget that. It *is* the end of the world!"

"You're really cheering me up a lot, you know that?"

"I'm sorry. I'd better get off the phone."

"Yes. You'd better. Thanks for asking me. It was a nice invitation."

"Sorry I laughed at you."

"That's okay. I have to get used to it. People are going to be laughing at me for the rest of my life."

"Well, try to cheer up a little, okay?"

"Okay."

"And try to stop sitting around, staring all the time."

"Okay."

"And one other thing."

"What's that?"

"Have a great time with Ramar! Ha-ha-ha-ha!"

Slam!

CHAPTER 31

Toby Calls Julie Again

"Hello?"

"Hello, Mrs. Reynolds?"

"No. It's Julie. Hi, Toby."

"Are you cheered up at all?"

"No."

"Good."

"Good? What's that supposed to mean?"

"Good means good."

"What's the matter with you?"

"Nothing's the matter with me. What's the matter with you?"

"Toby, you know what's the matter with me. Why are you doing this? What's gotten into you? Why are you being so mean?"

"You lied to me, Julie."

"Lied? Get real. I didn't."

"You did."

"Didn't."

"You said you couldn't go to the stupid homecoming dance with me because you already had a date. With Ramar."

"Right. I remember what I said, Toby. It was just a few hours ago. And it was the truth."

"No, it isn't."

"Toby—"

"You don't have a date with Ramar."

"What are you saying? You're not making any sense!"

"You don't have a date with Ramar, because Diane does!"

"What?"

"She's up in her room crying about it right now."

"That's impossible."

"Impossible? Here. I'll hold the phone up. Listen. Do you hear her?"

"That awful wailing sound? Isn't that a police siren?"

"No. It's Diane. She's been wailing like that all afternoon."

"Because—"

"Because she has a date with Ramar to the dance."

"But—but—"

"So why did you lie to me, Julie?"

"I didn't."

"We've been friends for a long time, and we've always been real honest with each other. Maybe even too honest some of the time. But that's what I liked about you. I always knew you would tell me exactly what was on your mind, whether there was anything on your mind or not. But now—I don't know. Maybe

I shouldn't have asked you out. Maybe that's it. Maybe you just want us to stay friends, to keep things the way they've always been. But you could've said that to me. You could have told me the truth. You didn't have to make up a story about having a date with Ramar."

"What? I'm sorry, Toby. I wasn't listening. I was thinking. What were you saying again?"

"What?"

"I said I didn't hear you. I was thinking about Ramar."

"Why did you lie to me, Julie? Just tell me that."

"I didn't lie. You have to believe me."

"Listen to those wails. Listen to that. Have you ever heard a more pitiful sound in your life?"

"No. No, I haven't."

"Those are the sounds of someone who has a date with Ramar."

"True. True. But I didn't lie to you. There's something strange going on here. Did Ramar call Diane to ask her out?"

"How should I know? She isn't speaking to me, remember? She isn't speaking to anyone now. She's just wailing at the top of her lungs. She was rolling around on the carpet before, but she stopped. I think she was picking up too much lint."

"That's awful. I'm very confused."

"I'm confused, too, Julie. And I'm really hurt. If you didn't want to go out with me, you could've said so. You didn't have to make up a lie, especially such a dumb one."

"It wasn't dumb!"

"But it was a lie? You admit it?"

"No! It wasn't! Ramar called me. He asked me to the dance. I said no a thousand times. He said fine, he'd pick me up two hours early. He said something about wearing the same fabric I wore so we'd match. It was a date, Toby, a real date. Something like that is too hideous to make up."

"Listen to Diane. I think she's started rolling around again."

"Hey, maybe this is good news!"

"Good news? What are you talking about?"

"Maybe I'm off the hook! Maybe Ramar has decided he likes Diane better. Maybe he made the date with her and plans to cancel his date with me! Maybe—"

"Maybe you'll need a new excuse not to go out with me?"

"Yeah. Maybe."

"I asked for that one, didn't I! What are you going to do?"

"Call Ramar."

"Call Ramar and?"

"And ask him if our date is still on. He'll say no. He's asked Diane out instead. And then I'll go with you."

"Well, that sounds pretty good to me. But what about poor Diane?"

"She'll get over it."

"Bye, Julie."

"Bye."

CHAPTER 32

Julie Calls Ramar

"Hello?"

"Hello, Ramar?"

"No. This is Mick. Hold on. I'll get him."

"Hello, please?"

"Ramar?"

"The very same. And whom do I have the pleasure of addressing?"

"This is Julie. Julie Reynolds."

"How are you today? Are you keeping your eye on the ball?"

"What?"

"That's an American expression I picked up. I believe it is called teenage slang. Did I pronounce it correctly?"

"My eye on the ball?"

"Oh. You say it, too. How charming!"

"Listen, Ramar—"

"In my country, we have a very different expression. We say, are you keeping the elephant in the cheese? I believe it means much the same thing."

"Probably. That's very interesting."

"Thank you, I'm sure. I would like to teach you many expressions from my country, and I hope you will teach me to say some of your favorites. I like to rap. Do you like to rap?"

"Uh—I'm not sure. Listen, Ramar—"

"If you can't take the heat, go bathe in the river."

"What?"

"Another popular expression I picked up."

"Very clever."

"Thank you, I'm sure."

"Ramar, did you ask me to the homecoming dance a few days ago?"

"Yes, indeed it was my supreme pleasure. I await the day with bird flutterings in my stomach."

"We *do* have a date for the dance?"

"Let there be no doubt. You may rest easy, my flower."

"And what about Diane Clarke? Have you by any chance spoken to her about the dance?"

"Yes, I most enthusiastically have."

"What? What do you mean? You have a date with Diane for the dance, too?"

"Yes, most agreeably. She asked me, and I accepted."

"Huh? She asked you?"

"Yes, to my endless delight and gratification."

"Is this 'The Twilight Zone,' or what?"

"I do not understand that quaint phrase."

"Never mind. So you're telling me you have two dates for the dance."

"Yes. Only two. In my country, I would be laughed at for so small a party. But I am certain I can make do quite adequately with only two."

"I don't believe this!"

"Believe in sheep."

"What?"

"Believe in sheep. Do you know the meaning of that phrase? Sheep are so solid and woolly, you see. So we say believe in sheep. Is my meaning clear?"

"Everything is clear. You have two dates to the dance."

"Yes. Only two."

"No. This can't be happening. Ramar, I—I—"

"Speak, my flower. Your tongue enchants my ear."

"Don't you know anything about going out on dates in this country? Don't you know that you can't have two dates? Why are you doing this to me? Why? What have I ever done to you?"

"You're losing it, Julie."

"I don't care! I'll never be able to live this down! Never! I can't—Hey! What did you just say?"

"I said you're losing it."

"Ramar? You said—"

"Ha-ha-ha-ha!"

"Uh-oh. What's going on?"

"It's me. Mick."

"What?"

"It's not Ramar. You haven't been talking to Ramar. It's been me the whole time."

"You?"

"Yeah. Pretty good imitation, huh?"

"You've been imitating Ramar? But I thought—"

"Ha-ha! I sure had you going. I sound just like him, don't I?"

"Yes. Just like him."

"Well, I've been listening to him since September. I pick up voices pretty easy. I've always been pretty good at imitating people."

"How terrific for you."

"Aw, don't get bitter. I was just goofing on you. That's only the second time I've tried my Ramar impression. You impressed?"

"The second time? What was the first time?"

"When your pal Diane called."

"Diane called you and you pretended to be Ramar?"

"Yeah. Ha-ha-ha."

"That's awful!"

"Yeah. Isn't it? It was just a little joke to pay her back."

"Pay her back? For what?"

"For hanging up on me. I called and asked her out. She slammed the phone down in my ear. So when she called back, I thought I'd do my Ramar and pay her back."

"And now she thinks she has a date to the homecoming dance with Ramar."

"I know. It's a riot, huh?"

"For sure. A riot. She's home crying her eyes out."

"Really?"

"Really."

"I guess my Ramar impression is even better than I thought."

"Well, what about me, Mick?"

"What about you?"

"Was that Ramar who called me a few days ago, or was it you pretending to be Ramar?"

"Bad news, kid."

"Bad news?"

"It was Ramar."

"I was afraid you were going to say that. So I have a date with Ramar."

"Right."

"And Diane thinks she has a date with Ramar, but she really doesn't."

"You're two for two."

"That isn't fair, is it?"

"Life's tough. Listen, when you dance with him, don't stand too close."

"Don't worry!"

"No. I'm serious. He wears these open-toed sandals, see. And he doesn't trim his toe nails. They stick out about six inches and they're real pointy."

"Now I'm totally depressed all over again. Thanks, Mick."

"Any time."

"Guess I'll get off the phone."

"Well, keep the elephant in the cheese. Hee-hee!"

"Very good. You sound just like him."

"Thanks. Bye, Julie."

"Bye."

═══ CHAPTER 33 ═══
Julie Calls Toby

═══

"Hello?"

"Hi, Mr. Clarke. Is Toby there?"

"Julie, it's me."

"Oh. Sorry. Your voice sounded so deep."

"I have a cold. What are you saying? That I normally have a high, squeaky voice?"

"Haven't you ever wondered why only dogs listen to you?"

"Julie—"

"I didn't say anything about your voice. Are you getting a little paranoid, or what?"

"No. I'm just a little down, that's all. My head is throbbing. My nose is dripping like a faucet. My glands are—"

"Okay. You have a cold, Toby. You really don't have to describe it, do you? I just ate dinner."

"Excuse me. I didn't mean to be gross."

"You never mean to be gross. You can't help it! Ha-ha!"

"You called to cheer me up, I guess."

"As a matter of fact."

"You're doing a heckuva job."

"As a matter of fact, you're going to thank me for this call."

"Thank you."

"Not yet. Wait till you hear what you have to thank me for."

"The suspense is killing me."

"Toby, stop being such a drip."

"A *drip?* Is that a new vocabulary word for you?"

"Don't be ridiculous. I'm sure lots of people have called you a drip."

"Thank you again."

"Are you going to shut up and listen to me so you can start thanking me properly?"

"Okay. I'm all ears."

"I know. You should have those fixed! Ha-ha!"

"You're just a barrel of laughs tonight. Notice how I'm not yucking it up too much?"

"Just shut up. I'm going to make you a hero."

"A sandwich? I already ate."

"Not funny. Listen to me. How would you like to be on Diane's good list again?"

"I wouldn't mind."

"Better than that. How would you like Diane to forgive you for the Mick Wilson trick you played on her, and be grateful to you forever, and think you're the greatest brother a girl ever had, and probably be your slave for the rest of your life?"

"Interesting. Very interesting. I suppose you're going to tell me how to do all that?"

"Yes. In fact, I'm going to tell you how to do all that without doing anything at all."

"Oh, right. For sure. And then you're going to tell me how to flap my arms and fly to the moon."

"Okay. Be Mr. Sarcastic. We can forget the whole thing."

"Sorry. Hold on a minute. I have to blow my nose."

Honnnnnnk!

"Toby, that was gross! You didn't have to blow your nose right into the phone. You did that deliberately."

"That wasn't the gross part. The gross part was that I didn't have a tissue! Ha-ha!"

"Very funny. For a two-year-old. Now, do you want me to tell you how to become a hero to Diane or not?"

"Of course I do. Shoot."

"Just tell her you'll get her out of her date with Ramar."

"What?"

"You heard me. Just tell her that."

"And then what do I do? How do I get her out of the date?"

"Just as I told you. By doing absolutely nothing."

"Go lie down, Julie. The fever must be very high. Put a cold cloth to your head. I'll call the doctor."

"Listen to me, pinhead. You can get Diane out of her date with Ramar by doing nothing—because she doesn't *have* a date with Ramar!"

"Huh?"

"Mick played a trick on her. He does a perfect imitation of Ramar. He pretended to be Ramar when she called and made her think she had a date to the dance with Ramar. But she doesn't."

"And you don't, either? That's great news!"

"No. Not such great news. I talked to the real Ramar. I have a date with him. Diane doesn't."

"Oh."

"Very eloquent. You shouldn't blow your nose so hard. You're losing brain cells."

"Give me a break. Let me get this straight. I go to Diane. I tell her how bad I feel that she's so miserable. I promise to get her out of her date with Two Ton. Then I do nothing at all. Then she's grateful to me for the rest of my life."

"You've got it, Ace. Now say thank you."

"Thank you, Julie."

"Hey, not bad. That sounded almost sincere."

"It was sincere. Thank you. I really mean it. Thank you for me. Thank you for Diane. I just wish—"

"What? That I could get out of *my* date so easily?"

"I just wish that I could repay you somehow. But you know what? I'm *going* to repay you. I'm going to get you out of your date so you can go to the dance with me. I'm going to straighten everything out with everyone. I'm going to see to it that there are no more jokes and tricks and that everyone is happy. That's what I'm going to do. What do you say to that?"

"Go lie down. Put a cool cloth to your head. I'll call the doctor."

"What's the matter? Don't you trust me?"

"About as far as I can throw you. I've got to get off the phone now."

"Thanks again."

"Go be a hero."

"Okay. I will." *Honnnnnnnk.*

"How gross!"

═══ CHAPTER 34 ═══

Toby Calls Diane

───────

"Hello?"

"Hello, Diane?"

"No, it's Francine."

"Hi, Francine. Is my sister over there?"

"Yeah. She's here."

"Is she still wailing and crying?"

"She's all cried out, Toby. She's into moaning now, and rolling her eyes."

"Isn't she overdoing it a bit?"

"You know Diane. She's a redhead. She can't help it."

"Could you ask her to come to the phone?"

"*Diane—it's your brother!* She says she doesn't want to talk to you, Toby."

"Francine, tell her she wants to talk to me. Tell her I'm about to change her life."

"Hello?"

"Hi, Diane."

"What do you want?"

"Don't be so nasty. I'm about to give you a reason to go on living."

"You're moving out of the house?"

"I'm going to pretend you didn't say that."

"I'm going to pretend you didn't call me, and I'm going to hang up in two seconds. I really don't see why—"

"Diane, I got you out of your date with Ramar."

"What?"

"I got you out. No date."

"No date?"

"No date."

"But—but—Toby, I don't know what to say. That's the nicest thing you've ever done for me."

"Yes, it is, isn't it."

"How did you do it?"

"It wasn't easy."

"How did you ever get through to Ramar? How did you make him understand you?"

"I just kept at it. I knew what it meant to you, Diane. I saw how upset you were, and I just couldn't allow it. So I did what I had to do. It was tough, but I did it. For you."

"Thank you. I mean—thank you! I'm so happy! What a nice thing to do. You're a great brother, Toby. I take back all of the 3,400,625 rotten things I've said about you!"

"Thanks, Diane. That's real big of you. Glad to know you were keeping count."

"I'll do anything for you, Toby. Anything at all. I'll be your slave. I can't thank you enough."

"Well, actually, there is something you can do."

"Name it. I mean it. Just name it."

"Well—this is going to sound a little strange, but bear with me. Can you talk real whispery like Jennifer Exley?"

"What?"

"You know the way she talks, sort of kittenish, really sexy."

"You mean like this?"

"Yes! Perfect! That's perfect!"

"Glad you like it."

"Yes. Keep it up. That's terrific. Now I need you to do a little favor for me. I'd like to play a little trick on Jennifer."

"Great! I've never been able to stand that snob."

"Good. All I want you to do is pretend to be Jennifer and call up Ramar in your sexy, whispery voice."

"Yes?"

"And ask Ramar to be your date to the homecoming dance."

"Gee, I don't know, Toby. I really don't want to talk to Ramar ever again. I get the deep shudders just thinking of him. I start to itch all over."

"Come on. You said you'd do anything for me. Besides, you won't be calling as you. You'll be calling as Jennifer."

"Oh, I don't know . . ."

"You can do it. I know you can. You've *got* to do it."

"Well, okay. Actually, it might be fun. But, wait— what if Mick answers? I'm too embarrassed to talk to Mick."

"He probably won't answer. And if he does, you're not you—you're Jennifer, remember?"

"Oh. Right. Okay. I'll do it. *I'm coming, Francine!* Talk to you later, Toby. And thanks again. Thanks, thanks, thanks."

"Don't thank me, Diane. Really. It was nothing."

═══ CHAPTER 35 ═══
Toby Calls Mick

"Hello?"

"Hello, Mick? This is Toby."

"No. This is Mick's dad. I don't know if Mick is home or not. He's supposed to be at practice. Do you want to speak to Ramar instead?"

"Oh, no. No. Please—no."

"Oh, wait. Mick is still here. *Mick, phone for you!*"

"Hello?"

"Hi, Mick. It's Toby. Toby Clarke."

"Yeah?"

"Yeah. Hi."

"I don't need any subscriptions to *Boys' Life*. Thanks, anyway."

"Funny. Very funny."

"Listen, Tobe. I'm late for practice, so make it quick, okay? Is this call part of your psych experiment?"

"Psych experiment? What are you talking about? I don't take psych. I took it last year."

"Oh. Guess I was mixed up. I thought all of these calls I've been getting were part of a psych experiment."

"No. That's sort of what I was calling about, though. My sister Diane—"

"Yeah. I know your sister. She hung up on me the other day."

"She didn't mean to."

"It sounded like she meant to. There was a definite slam, and then a dial tone. It sounded to me like she meant it."

"She didn't. I mean, she didn't know what she was doing. She didn't know who it was."

"I told her who it was."

"But she didn't believe you."

"She gets a lot of guys calling and saying they're Mick Wilson?"

"No, but she thought it was a trick."

"I don't know your sister. Why would I play a trick on her?"

"Because *I* played a trick on her, so she thought you were playing a trick on her."

"Yeah. Right. That makes sense. Well, I *did* play a trick on her. But that was after she hung up on me."

"I know. But that's not why I'm calling."

"I know why you're calling, Tobe. You're trying to get into *The Guinness Book of World Records* for the longest phone call without saying anything."

"No. I'm sorry, Mick. I'll get to the point."

"The point is on top of your head. Ha-ha!"

"Good one, Mick. Very good. My point is that

Diane didn't mean to hang up on you. And if you call her again and ask her to the dance, I think she'll be real happy."

"No tricks?"

"No. No tricks. We're even, remember? I'm not going to play any more tricks. On you."

"You sure?"

"Yes. I'm sure."

"Well—I might call your sister. Is she standing right there listening to this?"

"No. Of course not. She doesn't know I'm calling. She'd *die* if she knew. But I just wanted to help out. You know, clear things up. She felt terrible when she realized it was really you calling her. And she was too embarrassed to call you back."

"Yeah, well. I've got to run. I'm really late. Coach is going to use me for a backboard."

"Sorry. I'll get off. See you around."

"Not if I see you first. Ha-ha!"

"Bye, Mick."

"Hey, Tobe—one more thing."

"What's that?"

"Say hi to Jennifer Exley for me, okay? And give her a big kiss! Ha-ha-ha-ha! Later."

CHAPTER 36

Mick Calls Diane

"Hello?"

"Hello, Diane?"

"No. It's Francine. Hold on a minute. *Diane—it's for you. It's a boy!*"

"Hello?"

"Diane?"

"Yes?"

"It's Mick Wilson."

"Mick? Really?"

"Don't hang up! Ha-ha-ha!"

"No. I wouldn't. I mean, I won't. Wasn't that awful? What a mix-up!"

"Yeah. I guess."

"I'm really sorry."

"Yeah. Me, too."

"I really didn't know it was you."

"Yeah. I kind of figured."

"Shut up, will you? I'm trying to talk!"

"What?"

"No. Not you. Francine keeps asking me questions."

"Oh. I see. Well—"

"I was at the Grandview game last night."

"You were? We were robbed. We shouldn't have lost that one."

"But you were really good."

"I had a good shooting night, but my *D* fell off."

"What? Your *what* fell off?"

"My defense. That guy Harris got around me like I was invisible or something."

"Oh. Well—I thought you were good. You didn't deserve to foul out, either."

"Yeah. Tell me about it. The guy stepped on my foot and all I did was give him a little shove, and they call me on it."

"It wasn't fair."

"Hey, I didn't know you were a basketball fan."

"Yes. Well, I like going to the games. I'm a pretty good player, too. We'll have to play a little one-on-one sometime. I'll give you a few pointers."

"After last night, maybe I could use some. Ha-ha! Listen, I didn't call to talk basketball."

"Really?"

"I wondered if maybe you still didn't have a date. You know, to the dance."

"Well, no. Actually, I still don't."

"Well, if I asked you to go with me, what would you

do—tell me to stop putting you on and then hang up on me?"

"Why don't you try me?"

"Okay. I'll give it a try. Do you want to go to the dance with me?"

Slam!

CHAPTER 37

Diane Calls Mick

"Hello?"

"Gotcha!"

"Diane?"

"Ha-ha-ha-ha! That was just a joke! I couldn't resist!"

"Ha-ha! Funny. You got me, okay. I was kind of in shock. I just sat here, staring at the phone."

"Well, I had to pay you back for your Ramar imitation."

"You know all about that, huh?"

"Yes. I do. And it wasn't funny."

"Maybe it was a little funny?"

"About as funny as a toothache."

"That funny, huh?"

"Well, I got you back. Now we're even. I won't do it again. I promise. And, yes. I'd love to go to the dance with you."

"Yeah?"

"Yeah."

"Well, okay. I'm glad."

"I'm glad, too, Mick."

"No more tricks?"

"No more tricks."

"Okay. I've got to go mow the lawn. See you, Diane."

"See you, Mick. Thanks again."

"Well, bye."

"Bye. You hang up first."

"What?"

"Hang up first. I don't want you to think I'm hanging up on you again."

"Well, okay. Here goes."

Click.

=== CHAPTER 38 ===
Diane Calls Ramar

"Hello?"

"Hello, Ramar?"

"No. This is Mick's dad. Hold on. Are you sure you want Ramar?"

"Yes. I'm sure."

"Just checking. Hold on."

"Hello, please?"

"Ramar?"

"Yes, in the flesh. Hee-hee."

"I don't think you know me. My name is Jennifer Exley."

"You have a lovely voice, Jennifer. Like spring breezes blowing gently through the slag heaps."

"Why, thank you. What a nice compliment."

"Do you like herring?"

"Herring? No. I—"

"The softness of your voice reminded me of the

wind blowing the sails of the herring boats in my country. Oh boy, what a stench! It smells for many miles."

"Ramar, I—"

"Are you familiar with my country?"

"No. I don't think so."

"It is the yellow island on the map. Next to the bright pink island that's shaped like a goat's kidney."

"Oh, yes. I know which one you mean."

"You do?"

"Ramar, I've noticed you in school."

"I am much flattered. As we say in my country, the swine stands out from the pack of weasels. Ha-ha! It is very witty, I believe."

"Yes, very. I think you definitely stand out, too. I mean, it's hard not to notice you. I mean—"

"Now I must be thanking you for the compliment."

"Oh, it's nothing. I—uh—I'm very impressed with you. I think you must be an interesting person."

"I am but a humble dude, as I believe you say in America."

"Ramar, do you have a date to the homecoming dance?"

"Yes, thank you. I do. The young lady's name is Julie."

"Julie? Really? Oh. Well—do you think you could —uh—break your date with Julie? I really would like you to go with me."

"Okay. I will do it. I will not disappoint you."

"Wow. You didn't have to think about that for too long."

"I believe I noticed the tiniest bit of reluctance on Julie's part. I do not believe she will be very much brokenhearted. And I must say, your soft voice in my ear is—how do you say it in your colorful slang— driving me to bananas!"

"Ha-ha-ha! Thank you, Ramar. So—do you and I have a date?"

"In all certainty. I will arrange to disattach myself from Julie. I will pick you up three hours early so that we may become better acquainted before our date begins."

"How very thoughtful of you, Ramar."

"As we say in my country, the cow is thoughtful before the ax cuts off her head."

"I can't wait to hear more of your expressions. I hope you have a lot of them."

"I have a few."

"Well, see you soon."

"Yes, Jennifer. Your call has filled my heart. My limbs are shaking in anticipation."

"What a picture! Bye for now, Ramar."

"Bye, Jennifer."

CHAPTER 39

Diane Calls Toby

"Hello?"

"Hello, Toby?"

"You have reached the Clarke residence, but no one is home to answer the phone. Please leave a message at the sound of the beep, and we'll call you back as soon as we can."

Beeeep.

"Toby, are you home? Come on. Pick up the phone. Aren't you there? No? Well, okay. I'm at Francine's. I just wanted to tell you I played your little joke on Ramar. I was great! I sounded just like Jennifer, and Ramar fell for me like a ton of bricks. Or should I say, like *two* tons of bricks!

"You didn't tell me that Julie had a date with him. Why did you leave that little detail out? I wonder. Anyway, she doesn't have a date with him anymore. Jennifer Exley does. I guess Julie will be a happy person now.

"You certainly are Mr. Fix-It these days, Toby. You fixed things for me, too. And guess what? Mick Wilson called and asked me to the dance. I guess maybe you had something to do with that, too. Thanks, Tobe. I really mean it. You're going to go to heaven with your shoes on. You've done so many good deeds this week, maybe you should've been a Boy Scout!

"I guess everyone is happy now. I know Julie will be. I'm going to give her a call and patch things up with her. Why not? It was all just a big mix-up. And I'm happy, too. I guess the only one who'll be unhappy is Jennifer. But she deserves it. She's such a money-hungry snob.

"Anyway, that's my message, Tobe. It was nice chatting with you like this. See you at dinner. And thanks again. Bye.

"Be sure to erase this tape when you get home. I don't think mom and dad would understand it, do you? I'm not sure if I understand it, either. Bye."

CHAPTER 40
Toby Calls Julie

"Hello?"

"Hello, Julie?"

"No. This is her dad."

"Oh. Sorry, Mr. Reynolds. You didn't sound like you."

"I sounded like a girl?"

"No. Sorry. I—I was just expecting Julie to answer."

"Hold on. I'll get her."

"Hello?"

"Well, it's all fixed."

"What's fixed?"

"Everything. I fixed everything."

"Congratulations. Now get your head fixed. You're not making any sense."

"Is that your idea of wit? Well, you're *half* right!"

"Toby, if I'm a half-wit, you're a nitwit! Ha-ha!"

"You really think that's funny, don't you? It's pitiful! I'm fifteen years old, and I've never heard anything so feebleminded."

"Fifteen? Is that your age or your I.Q.? Ha-ha-ha!"

"Just shut up, Julie."

"Who's going to make me?"

"I'm going to make you."

"How?"

"I'm going to tell you how I got you out of your date with Ramar."

"You what? You did?"

"I knew that would shut you up."

"Toby, I'm sorry. Really. I take everything back. Did you really—"

"It hasn't been easy, but I got everything straightened around. Diane is going out with Mick. And—"

"She told me. She called me a few hours ago. We made up. We're best friends again. It was all just a silly mix-up."

"And I paid Jennifer Exley back by getting her a date with Ramar."

"Diane told me that, too. That's a riot."

"So all of the practical jokes and tricks are over, and we can—"

"Yes. Diane told me."

"Well, I guess Diane told you everything I had to say."

"I guess she did."

"Uh—did she tell you I'd still like you to go to the homecoming dance with me?"

"No. She didn't mention that."

"That's why I did all that, you know."

"What?"

"Got everything straightened out with everyone so that you could go to the dance with me."

"How sweet."

"I know we've sort of been friends for a long time. But I think maybe we could get to be more than friends."

"Maybe—"

"So? How about it, Julie? Will you go to the dance with me?"

"No. I don't think so."

"What?"

"Just joking, Toby. Just joking. Of course I'll go with you."

"Whew. Hey, Julie—do me a favor?"

"What's that?"

"No more jokes. At least for a while."

"Okay. That seems like a good idea. Maybe we should stop talking on the phone so much. It only seems to lead to trouble."

"Stop talking on the phone? But—"

"Maybe you could come over. We could see each other in person. I live right across the street, after all."

"Uh—yeah. That's a great idea, Julie. I'd like that."

"Good."

"Well, okay. Guess I should get off the phone. See you."

"Oh, Toby? One more thing."

"Yes?"

PHONE CALLS

"Those chemistry notes? Could I borrow them again?"

"Sure. Want me to bring them over?"

"Yes."

"I'll be right over. Bye."

"Bye, Toby."

EPILOGUE

Ramar Calls Jennifer

"Hello?"

"Hello. Do I have the pleasure of speaking into the ear of Jennifer Exley?"

"No. This is the maid. Just a second."

"Hello?"

"Hello, this is Ramar."

"Ramar? I'm sorry. I couldn't possibly know anyone with that name. I think you have the wrong number."

"No. This is Ramar. I am calling for you, Jennifer. Once again I am hearing the soft sounds you make like tree frogs ceaselessly rubbing their hind legs."

"What is this? A gag?"

"No, it is Ramar."

"Ramar—oh! The foreign exchange student. Oh. Right. Now, I remember. How could I forget?"

"And for me as well. How can I forget the whisper

of your voice as you made such an exciting invitation to this humble dude."

"Invitation?"

"To the dance on Saturday eve."

"I invited you to the homecoming dance? I suddenly don't feel well. Listen, this is impossible—"

"Yes. We can do the impossible. As we say in my country, two heads are more impossible than one. I am calling only to confirm the time that I may fly to your side."

"You? Fly? Can you fit in a plane?"

"What? There is static on the line."

"Ramar, listen to me. You are mistaken. I will not—I cannot go to the dance—"

"I am eager to tell you of my exciting news. My father wrote to me this day and enclosed photographs of our newest castle."

"Your castle?"

"It is our third. You are probably surprised. But in my country, royalty is expected to spend its fortune on castles for the glory of the people."

"What? Royalty? What did you say about royalty?"

"I have not let it be known among my American friends, who are well-meaning but lowly peasants. My true name is Prince Ramar the Twelfth. I am of the royal family in my country and upon my return shall inherit the throne."

"You're going to be a king? And you have a castle?"

"Three castles. Please do not think me boastful. It would be in shocking bad taste, I believe, to boast of my family or of my family's vast fortune. As we say in my country, the wagging tongue of a boastful man risks getting sunburnt."

"Royalty? A fortune? I had no idea you were such an interesting person, Ramar. I don't exactly know how this happened, but I think maybe we have a date to the dance after all. I'll be delighted to go with you. Why don't you pick me up at eight? And be sure to bring those photos of your castle."

"My heart will be flopping about in my shirt pocket until then, my flower."

"Ha-ha! I just love your cute expressions. You're such a cute guy."

"Ha-ha. Thank you, Jennifer. You are cute, too. As cute as a bug under the sink, as you Americans say."

"See you Saturday night, Ramar. Bye-bye."

"Bye-bye, Jennifer. I will be there with bells on."

"I sure hope that's just an expression."

ABOUT THE AUTHOR

R. L. STINE is the author of more than 70 books of humor, adventure and mystery for young readers.

For ten years he was the editor of *Bananas,* a national humor magazine for young people. In addition to magazine and book writing, he is currently Head Writer of the children's TV show "Eureeka's Castle."

He lives in New York City with his wife Jane and son Matthew.